# HARLEQUIN®
## *Presents~*

A warm welcome to all our readers; it's cold outside, but the books Harlequin Presents has got for you in January will leave you positively glowing!

Raise your temperature with two right royal reads! *The Sheikh's Innocent Bride,* by top author Lynne Graham, whisks you away to the blazing dunes of the desert in a classic tale of a proud sheikh's desire for the young woman employed to clean his castle. Meanwhile, Robyn Donald is back with another compelling Bagaton story in *The Royal Baby Bargain,* the latest installment in her immensely popular New Zealand-based BY ROYAL COMMAND miniseries.

Want the thermostat turned up? Then why not travel with us to the glorious Greek islands, where *Bought by the Greek Tycoon,* by favorite author Jacqueline Baird, promises searing emotional scenes and nights of blistering passion, and Susan Stephens's *Virgin for Sale*—the first title in our steamy new miniseries UNCUT—sees an uptight businesswoman learning what it is to feel pleasure in the hands of a *real* man!

For Cathy Williams fans, there's a new winter warmer: in *At the Italian's Command,* the heart of a notoriously cool, workaholic tycoon is finally melted by a frumpy but feisty journalist. And try turning the pages of rising star Melanie Milburne's latest release—*Back in her Husband's Bed,* about a marriage rekindled in sunny Sydney, Australia, is *almost* too hot to handle!

For a full list of titles and book numbers, see inside the front cover (opposite)—and enjoy!

# Melanie Milburne

## BACK IN HER HUSBAND'S BED

Bedded by...

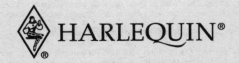

*Forced to bed...then to wed?*

## HARLEQUIN®

TORONTO • NEW YORK • LONDON
AMSTERDAM • PARIS • SYDNEY • HAMBURG
STOCKHOLM • ATHENS • TOKYO • MILAN • MADRID
PRAGUE • WARSAW • BUDAPEST • AUCKLAND

ISBN 0-373-12516-X

BACK IN HER HUSBAND'S BED

First North American Publication 2006.

This edition published by arrangement with Harlequin Books S.A.

® and TM are trademarks of the publisher. Trademarks indicated with
® are registered in the United States Patent and Trademark Office, the
Canadian Trade Marks Office and in other countries.

www.eHarlequin.com

**Printed in U.S.A.**

## All about the author...
### *Melanie Milburne*

Melanie read her first Harlequin novel when she was seventeen and has never looked back. She decided she would settle for nothing less than a tall dark handsome hero as her future husband. Well, she's not only still reading romance, but writing it as well! As for the tall dark handsome hero, she fell in love with him on the second date and was secretly engaged to him within six weeks!

They moved to Scotland so he could work and study for his M.D. in surgery, and two sons later, they arrived in Hobart, Tasmania—the jewel in the Australian crown. Once their boys were in school, Melanie went back to university and received her bachelor and then master's degree.

For her final assessment, she conducted a tutorial in literary theory concentrating on the romance genre. As she was reading a paragraph from the novel of a prominent Harlequin author the door suddenly burst open. The husband that she thought was working was actually standing there dressed in a tuxedo, his dark brown gaze centered on her startled blue one. He strode across the room, hauled Melanie into his arms and kissed her deeply and passionately before setting her back down and leaving without a single word. The lecturer gave Melanie a high distinction and her fellow students gave her jealous glares! You can see by now her pilgrimage into romance writing was more or less set!

Melanie also enjoys long-distance running and is a nationally ranked top-ten masters swimmer in Australia. She learned to swim as an adult, so for anyone who thinks they can't do something—you can! Her motto is Don't Say I Can't; Say I Can Try.

To Diane Perndt and Vicki Flukes.
Through all my thicks or thins, sinks or swims,
losses or wins—you two have been there to either
commiserate or celebrate with me.
Thank you.

# PROLOGUE

*The Creston Tower Hotel, Sydney,*
*Friday 13th September, 10:33 pm*

'MS GRESHAM!' A female journalist rushed at Carli with a microphone as soon as the lift doors were prised apart. 'Tell us about your experience of being trapped in a lift for more than two hours with your ex-husband, Xavier Knightly.'

'No comment,' Xavier answered for her, his hands tightening on Carli's arm as he led her determinedly through the small crowd of reporters.

'Ms Gresham?' The microphone swung back to Carli. 'Is it true you left your marriage to Xavier Knightly to pursue your own career in law?'

'Please get out of our way,' Xavier said curtly. 'We have nothing to say.'

'There was a lot of interest in the paper you delivered this afternoon, Ms Gresham,' the indomitable journalist continued. 'Have you anything further to add?'

'I—' Carli opened her mouth to answer but Xavier tugged her along with him down the hall and she had no choice but to follow him.

He shouldered open another exit door and led her up several flights of stairs, finally coming out on the Presidential level.

'Where are we going?' she asked somewhat breathlessly as she tried to match his long-strided pace.

'To my room to have that drink I promised you well

over two hours ago,' he answered grimly. 'I think I could safely say we're both in dire need of one.'

Carli was inclined to agree, although she didn't say it out loud as she waited for him to unlock the door. He held it open for her and she stepped through and looked around with interest, buying some time to get her rattled nerves under some sort of control.

'Nice suite.' She inspected the view over the city and harbour with a critical eye. 'We don't get this sort of luxurious comfort in steerage.'

She heard the slide of his silky tie as he removed it from the collar of his shirt and turned around to look at him. 'But then you always insisted on the best, didn't you?'

His dark blue eyes held hers. 'Do you have a problem with that?'

'No, not unless it comes at the expense of someone else.'

'I paid for the room in advance.'

'I didn't mean that and you know it.'

'Look, Carli, let's just drop the feminist crap for a while, OK? I asked you to have a drink with me, not to castrate me.'

She let out her breath on a gasp of indignation. 'Why is it men always think women are intent on emasculating them whenever we bring up the topic of equality?'

'I told you I don't wish to discuss it any further.'

'No, you wouldn't,' she sniped at him. 'It's far too comfortable at the top of the heap, isn't it? You wouldn't be interested in making room for anyone else way up there.'

'What would you like to drink?' He turned away to the mini-bar compartment, which incensed her even more; she didn't like being dismissed like a recalcitrant child. It was a skill he'd perfected in the three years they were married but somehow she found it even more annoying now.

'I don't want to have a drink.'

'Fine.' He poured himself one and sat on one of the sofas and began to drink it.

She shifted from one foot to the other, her eyes carefully avoiding his.

'The bathroom is through there.' He pointed behind her, lifting his glass to his mouth once more.

Carli swung away, striding off to where he'd directed, doing her best to ignore the expanse of his bed on her way to the huge *en suite*.

She took her time in the bathroom, washing her hands and finger-combing her wild chestnut hair so she didn't look quite so out of control, but no matter how hard she tried she couldn't quite erase the nervous, agitated look she could see reflected in her eyes.

Being trapped in a lift with the man you'd divorced five years ago was not to be recommended, she thought wryly. It had been bad enough knowing he was going to be at the same family-law conference as her, watching her, listening to her…hating her…

She drew in a calming breath and made her way back out to where Xavier was lounging, drink in hand, as if nothing unusual had occurred in the last hour or so.

'Changed your mind about that drink?' he asked.

'I think I'll have a glass of water.'

He put his drink down and got to his feet to get her what she'd requested. She watched him as he put some ice into a tall glass, pouring some bottled water into it before handing it to her. She took it with a murmur of thanks and began to drink it so she didn't have to converse with him.

She studied him over the top of her glass, taking in his tall, well-groomed features as if committing them to memory. His hair was still glossy black but there were a few strands of steel grey around his temples that hadn't been there five years ago. At thirty-six he was quite clearly a man who still enjoyed maintaining a high level of physical fitness. His stomach was flat and his muscles toned, his olive skin tanned in spite of the unusually cold winter Sydney had recently experienced. His clothes were always of the highest quality and although his shirt was undone at the collar and the cuffs at his strong wrists were rolled back casually, the fabric still spoke of a well-known designer.

He was the epitome of the successful man. Power, riches and privilege were things he took more or less for granted. His reputation as a family-law-court lawyer was well known in all legal circles, even those as far out west as hers. The common catchphrase associated with him was 'get him and get even'. With Xavier Knightly acting for you, back-up wasn't necessary. He was a veritable army of knowledge and expertise and many of his colleagues had to think twice before taking him on in opposition, knowing how good he was at court-room showdowns.

She met his watchful gaze across the room and couldn't quite help the instinctive sucking in of her breath at the mere sight of him. She had known every millimetre of his six-foot-four body, had heard him in the throes of passion and in the maelstrom of anger. They had shared so much but in the end it hadn't been enough…

'Come and sit down,' he said. 'And for God's sake would you please stop scowling at me?'

'I'm not scowling.'

'Yes, you are. You have your all-men-are-bastards look on your face.'

'That's ridiculous.' She sat down heavily and glared at him.

'There,' he pointed at her, 'you're doing it now—scowling.'

She couldn't stop the bubble of laughter at his imitation of her expression. 'I'm not that bad, surely!'

His mouth tilted into a lazy smile as he looked across at her. 'You look absolutely beautiful when you laugh. I'd forgotten just how beautiful.'

She felt the colour staining her cheeks and hastily lowered her eyes.

'Look at me, Carli.'

She raised her face to look at him and her heart squeezed at the thought of never seeing those dark blue eyes again.

He'd promised one drink and no further contact.

This was it—the final curtain on their troubled relationship.

The end.

'I should go.' She got to her feet and put her glass on the table. 'We said one drink and I—'

Xavier was on his feet and blocking her exit before she had even finished her sentence.

'No.'

She gave him a nervous glance. 'What do you mean…no?'

'I'm about to have dinner,' he said. 'I know it's late but why not join me?'

'Dinner?' She frowned.

'You have something against food?'

'No…but you and me and dinner isn't really a good combination,' she pointed out. 'We'll probably argue and embarrass the other diners.'

'There won't be any other diners if we eat in here by ourselves,' he said.

She should have seen that coming and was irritated with herself for falling so neatly into the snare he'd so expertly laid.

'I'm not hungry.'

'You're too thin.'

'You're too arrogant!' she shot back.

'Now you're being too sensitive.'

'And you are being a complete and utter jerk!' She backed away as he came closer. 'What are you doing?' She held up her hands as if to hold him off.

'If you insist on leaving now then I insist on one last kiss.'

She ran her tongue over her dry lips as the backs of her knees met the edge of the sofa. 'I don't want to kiss you,' she said but her tone lacked the strength of conviction she so desperately needed.

'Is that the truth and nothing but the truth, so help you God?'

'Don't play your court-room games with me, Xavier. I came up here for a drink and nothing else and you damn well know it.'

'One kiss, Carli, for old times' sake.'

She knew enough about his mouth to know one kiss would never be enough to satisfy her and she had to avoid it at all costs.

'I have to go…' She edged away from the sofa and made to brush past him but his hands came down on her shoulders and turned her effortlessly to face him.

'Why so afraid?' His dark eyes burned into hers.

'I'm not…' She took a lumpy swallow. 'I just don't think we should re-plough old fields, that's all.'

A heavy, pulsing silence began to throb between them.

Carli found her gaze slipping to his mouth almost of its own volition. Her heart began to hammer behind her already tightening breasts, and her legs turned traitor on her by weakening beneath her like dampened paper. She saw his head coming towards her in slow motion but she didn't move out of his reach. She felt like a light-blinded animal caught by the high beam of a car as it steadily approached.

She couldn't move even if she tried.

His mouth touched hers so softly she wondered if she'd imagined it, but then he did it again, this time a little firmer, and she felt her lips blaze with instant heat. He stroked his tongue along the cleft of her mouth and her lips parted on a soundless sigh, his entry into the cavern of her mouth sending her pulses skyrocketing out of control.

She felt his hands thread their way through the thick curtain of her hair in the same way he had used to do years ago, the simple action bringing her one step forward so their bodies touched from chest to thigh. She felt the unmistakable length of him swelling against her belly and her inner body responded as if he'd flicked a switch. She felt the silkiness of sensual need between her legs, and her resolve to resist him faded away to some far-away, unreachable place.

She kissed him back with all the pent-up despair of her loneliness over the time they'd been apart, her body aching for him with an intensity she knew she wouldn't be able to rein back in now it was finally set loose.

Her teeth found his bottom lip and dragged it into her mouth for her tongue to salve. She felt him jerk against her in reaction and couldn't help a tiny shiver of delight that even after all this time she could still affect him so.

His tongue tangled with hers, rasping over the smooth surface of her teeth to dip into the recesses of her mouth as if mimicking what his very male body had done repeatedly to her in the past.

Her body remembered with a heady rush of recognition, the blood flying through her veins as if in search of his touch on her skin. His mouth burned on hers, sending flames of desire to every secret place as if he were spreading a flammable liquid inside and over her. She erupted in a storm of need that could not be banked down no matter how hard she tried to contain it. She could feel the pull of desire like an irresistible lure being held in front of her. Nothing had prepared her for this conflagration of her senses. She was beyond thinking with his mouth on hers. She needed his touch, needed his need of her to remind her of all they had shared in the past, to remind her of what her life had once been when she'd been secure in his arms.

His mouth lifted off hers and although he didn't say a word his intimate question hung in the air between them all the same. She saw it reflected in his gaze as it secured hers, the silent message of desire being transmitted in crackling sparks that threatened to scorch her very soul.

She answered with her mouth as it returned to his, her arms going around his waist so her hands could dip to his buttocks and draw his heat even closer to her burning need.

He lifted her in his arms with his mouth still locked to hers and carried her to the bedroom, only breaking his kiss to put her down on the mattress. She watched as he removed his clothes with impatient hands, her own desire for him growing as every part of his leanly muscled body was revealed to her ravenous eyes.

He joined her on the bed and within the space of a few breathless seconds her clothes had joined his on the floor. The slide of his skin on hers was like a drug; she wanted him so much she could barely breathe without pain.

She refused to think about tomorrow and how she would feel after this brief encounter. She wanted him with a desperation she hadn't realised had been lurking silently inside her. Her inner emptiness began to ache with the need to be filled, and, when his hair-roughened thighs bound hers on either side in a muscled embrace, any last-minute chance of self-control finally slipped out of her grasp.

His hands shaped her breasts before he bent his mouth to taste her peaking flesh, his tongue rolling over each nipple until she couldn't stop a whimper of pleasure escaping through her kiss-swollen lips. He moved down from her breasts, lingering over her belly button, dipping his warm tongue in and out until she was squirming restlessly beneath him.

She sucked in a sharp little breath as he moved even lower, the caress of his breath between her legs sending her into a frenzy of anticipatory delight. She clutched at the bed covering beneath her hands, her fingers curling into the fabric to anchor her against the storm of feeling his slow-moving tongue was producing. Just when she thought she could stand it no more he moved over her to claim her mouth and his body slipped into place with one accurate thrust that sent another gasp from her mouth into the sexy saltiness of his.

It had been so long!

His body set a hard-paced rhythm which thrilled her, for it spoke of his urgent need. He was hot and hard and heavy within her but she relished in the hot lava flow of desire coursing through his body to scald hers. When he touched her intimately with his fingers to increase her pleasure she had to bite down on her lips to stop herself from crying out. He knew her body so well, what it wanted, what it needed and how it responded.

She felt the rolling wave hit her in a smashing blow that sent a kaleidoscope of fragmented colour through her brain, each tiny sparkle settling around her in the afterglow of release.

She felt him tense in preparation for his own supreme moment, his final surge splintering her with renewed feeling as he rocked against her, spilling himself into her warmth.

His large body gradually relaxed and she felt his warm, still hectic breath feathering along the sensitive skin of her neck. Her arms were around him, her hands moving over the smooth skin of his back in rediscovering exploratory movements.

'Was that too fast and furious for you?' He eased himself up on one elbow to look down at her, his night-sky eyes holding hers.

'We shouldn't have done it,' Carli said in instant self-reproach, hastily looking away.

'Probably not,' Xavier agreed with a wry smile, trailing a lazy, long, tanned finger down the length of her still quivering thigh. 'But given the circumstances it was more or less inevitable.'

'It is never a good idea for ex-partners to get involved again. It only causes confusion and further hurt.' She spoke through tightened lips, her breathing still not quite under control.

He rolled away and placed his arms behind his head, his gloriously naked body pulling her gaze back even though her common sense kept insisting she turn away.

'You sound as if you're reading that straight from a law textbook,' he chided. 'It was only sex, Carli—no big deal.'

'It's a big deal to me.'

He turned his head to look at her, his eyes very dark and intense. 'Are you saying you still feel something for me after all this time?'

'Of course not,' she said with a touch of tartness. 'You killed what I felt for you a long time ago.'

If he was disappointed with her answer he certainly didn't show it on his face. He simply laid back his head and crossed his legs at his ankles in a casual, unaffected pose, and her blood instantly began to boil.

She couldn't help feeling as if she'd been set up for a bit of ex-sex to pass the time. She should have known when she'd presented her paper on the obstacles young women in the legal field faced he'd be sitting in the third row from the back just waiting to pounce on her at question time. Their very public sparring match had no doubt all been part of the intellectual foreplay that had led to his little social-let's-try-and-be-civil-even-though-we're-now-divorced drink.

'My God, you planned this, didn't you?' She leapt off the bed in one movement and snatched up her clothes to cover herself.

He arched one dark brow at her. 'Your imagination is as usual working overtime.'

'Don't lie to me, you…you…bastard!' She zipped up her skirt and flung her arms through her blouse without bothering to replace her bra, which in the heat of the moment she had failed to find.

'You and your one drink and one kiss for old times' sake!' she railed at him as she stuffed her feet back into her high-heeled shoes. 'Do you think I'm so stupid to fall for that old routine?'

He gave her an ironic look. 'Apparently you just did.'

Her eyes scanned the room for something to throw at him. It wouldn't be the first time she tossed something his way, but this time there were no priceless Knightly heirloom vases at hand.

'I wouldn't if I were you,' he warned. 'You know the law well enough to know what happens to people who deface hotel rooms.'

'You arrogant, stuffed-shirt, male chauvinistic, opportunistic, calculating, conniving, vindictive, ruthless, arrogant—'

'You already said arrogant. Try to be original if you must flay me with such opprobrium.'

Carli was almost speechless with rage.

'I never want to see you again!' she screeched at him.

He held her fiery glare with consummate ease, his tone

even and cool. 'That was the deal, remember? You stated the terms yourself, Carli. One last drink and I promised never to see or speak to you ever again.'

'And I meant it!' She stamped her foot for emphasis. 'I never, ever want to see you again. Do you hear me?'

'Loud and clear.' His tone held its usual trace of mockery, which sent her fury up another dangerous notch.

'I hate you!' Carli flung at him bitterly. 'I *hate, hate, hate* you!'

'Just as well since you divorced me five years ago; what a waste of very commendable legal work it would be if you didn't.'

She swung away in case he caught sight of the tears shining in her eyes and stalked towards the door.

'Toss me the room-service menu on your way out, Carli,' he called out to her. 'After all that hot and sweaty exercise I'm feeling a little bit peckish.'

She turned back to face him and used a very unladylike expression to describe just exactly what he could do with the room-service menu.

His chuckle of laughter broke her fragile hold on her temper and she picked up the cardboard menu card and, tearing it into tiny shreds, stalked back across to where he was lying and threw them all over him like confetti.

'*Bon appétit.*' She dusted off her hands and stomped back to the door, slamming it so hard behind her the pictures hanging in the hall outside rattled in their gilt-edged frames.

Xavier listened to the staccato beat of her heels as she made her way down the hall, each and every footstep striking a painful nerve somewhere deep in the middle of his chest.

His fingers closed over the shredded menu card lying
around him on the bed and he bit out one hard, sharp,
unprintable word as he flung the pieces to the carpeted
floor…

# CHAPTER ONE

*Three months later...*

CARLI stared at the thin blue line in horror. 'Oh, my God!'

She clutched at the bathroom basin in much the same way she'd been doing on and off for weeks as she came to grips with the final devastating confirmation of her pregnancy.

The walls of the small room began to close in on her and she held on to consciousness with as much tenacity as she could.

Pregnant!

With Xavier's child!

She opened her eyes to inspect the testing kit once more but it was still the same colour.

She stumbled through to the bedroom, her body shivering in reaction rather than to cold.

It must be a mistake!

It *had* to be a mistake.

They'd only been together that one time and she had been sure she was in a safe period in her cycle, not that she'd really thought about it at the time.

She slammed her fist into her pillow and bit down on her bottom lip until she tasted blood.

She'd stormed from his hotel room vowing to never set eyes on him again, never imagining such a subsequent scenario as this! That one momentary lapse into passionate madness had set her world upside down.

She wouldn't tell him.

Oh, really, her conscience pricked her. What if he somehow found out? He's Sydney's best legal eagle. Don't forget: get him and get even. That was his credo and she knew he would just as easily apply it against her if pressed to do so.

OK, so she would tell him.

Yeah, right, as if he's going to accept the news with any sort of gladness.

'Oh, God!' She shut her eyes against the vision of his disdain. 'I can't do it! I just can't do it!'

Nausea rolled in her stomach and she made a desperate lunge for the bathroom, only just making it in time.

She lifted her pale face to meet her reflection in the mirror above the basin, shocked at her pallor and even more alarmed by the haunted, hollow look in her caramel-brown gaze.

It took Carli a further twenty-seven days before she garnered enough courage to do what had to be done. She gave her slightly protruding abdomen a nervous stroke as she approached the office tower where Xavier had his suite of offices. She hadn't phoned to announce her intention of seeing him. She hadn't trusted herself not to blurt her news over the line instead of face to face. Not that either way was going to make things any easier. He was going to be shocked and quite possibly furious as well. His shock she could deal with, but his anger?

She took the stairs and lost count after floor number ten. She traipsed on doggedly, step by agonising step, feeling like someone on their way up to the gallows.

'Mr Knightly is in court and won't be back until four this afternoon,' his middle-aged secretary announced in somewhat prim tones.

Carli's heart sank along with her courage. Could she wait

three hours? And more to the point, could she go through the ordeal of the fire escape one more time?

'Who will I say wants to see him?' the secretary asked, picking up a pen and a message pad.

'I…Car…Carli Gresham,' she said, knowing she wouldn't get an appointment without revealing her name.

'Carli as in Carla?' The secretary arched one pencilled brow at her.

'No,' she said. 'Carli as in Carli—trust me, he'll know exactly who it is.'

Xavier was the only person in the legal profession to call her Carli instead of Carla, and by the simple exchange of that one letter managed to strip away the thin veneer of sophistication she had fought so hard to keep in place.

The secretary took in her slightly flushed appearance and her austere manner visibly softened. 'Would you like a drink? Mr Knightly is often early from court when things go his way. You mightn't have such a long wait after all.'

Carli felt like asking: when did things ever not go Xavier Knightly's way? However, she refrained from doing so when she caught sight of a water-cooler machine in the waiting area.

The secretary noticed the line of her gaze and ushered her towards it with all the efficiency of a mother hen. 'Sit yourself down, Miss Gresham, and help yourself to a drink, or I could make you a coffee or tea instead?'

'No, thank you, water's fine, and it's Ms not Miss.'

'Yes, of course it is, how silly of me.'

Before Carli could ask her what she meant she'd bustled back to her credenza, bent her head to her computer and begun tapping away like a barnyard hen did at spilled wheat.

Carli couldn't help wondering how many secretaries Xavier had worked his way through over the last five years.

This one seemed a little more sensible than his usual type and she couldn't help wondering what had brought about the change.

She sighed and picked up a magazine, flicking through it without interest. From time to time she glanced at the clock on the wall but the minutes appeared to be crawling by at an evolving invertebrate's pace.

She felt her usual afternoon lethargy hit like a sledge-hammer and tried to keep her eyelids open but they felt weighted by anvils and she finally had to give in to the urge to close them.

The sofa she was sitting on was soft and comfortable and she settled into its leather cushions, promising herself she would shut her eyes for five minutes and five minutes only…

'How long has she been here?' Xavier asked his secretary in a deep undertone, a frown forming between his dark brows.

Elaine Johnston inspected the clock on the wall before answering in a sibilant whisper, 'Two and a half hours.'

He muttered a swear word under his breath. 'I could have been back an hour ago but I had a drink with one of the other lawyers.'

'Quite frankly I think she needed the sleep,' Elaine whispered back. 'She was very pale when she came in. Do you know her?'

'Know her?' He sent her an ironic glance. 'I was once married to her.'

Elaine's eyes went out on stalks. '*That's* your ex-wife?'

'Certainly is.'

His secretary's mouth opened and closed. 'What does she want to see you about?'

'Can't be about a divorce,' he said with a wry twist to his mouth. 'We've already had one of those.'

'If you ask me she looks rather fragile…' Elaine chewed the end of a pen thoughtfully.

'I didn't ask you, but believe me, she's a whole lot tougher than she looks.'

'Well, I think I'll leave you to it,' Elaine said, gathering up her things. 'I don't think I want to be witness to the sparks that might fly once you get her alone.'

Xavier didn't answer. He was still remembering the sparks that had flown the last time they were together, in fact had thought of little else in the four months since he'd last seen her. He'd thought of contacting her hundreds— no, thousands of times, but he'd promised her one drink and no further contact. And after she'd stormed out of his hotel room and left the conference before it was even over he'd had no choice but to assume she was perfectly content with the arrangement.

As if Carli sensed his presence she opened her eyes on his approach. She brushed back the hair off her face and slid her curled-up legs to the floor with a selfconscious adjustment of her long skirt and overflowing blouse as she stood up.

'Well, well, well,' he drawled. 'Look who's here.'

'I had to see you.' She didn't bother with a proper greeting, twisting her hands in front of her like a nervous school-girl.

'I'm sorry you had to wait,' he said, his tone belying the apology of his words. 'But I'm free now. Come into my office and let's get this over with.'

It wasn't a good start, she thought as she followed him down the capacious hall to his plush office. She could tell he wasn't in a good mood and what she had to tell him was hardly going to lighten it.

He held the door for her and she stepped through, trying not to notice how her skirt brushed along his thigh as she went past.

She went to the chair opposite his desk and sat down on the edge of it, her eyes following him as he took his place behind the expansive rectangle of highly polished timber.

He moved forward in his chair and, leaning his arms on his desk, made a steeple with his fingers. 'So, this must be pretty important. I thought you never wanted to see me again.' His eyes locked on to hers.

'It is important.' She ran her tongue over her dry lips. 'Extremely important.'

'Well?'

All her earlier rehearsals went out the window as she blurted, 'I'm pregnant.'

He didn't move a muscle.

'I fail to see what this has to do with me,' he said after a short pause. 'Do you want me to represent you legally to extract funds from the father for your child's upkeep?'

She swallowed the constriction in her throat.

'Who is the father by the way?' he added before she could find her voice. 'Anyone I might know?'

'As a matter of fact, yes.'

He leant back in his chair, his right thumb compressing the top of a pen, the tiny clicks sounding loud in the pulsing silence.

'He's…' She hesitated. How could she tell him without some sort of preamble?

'You seem to be having some trouble recalling his name,' he observed. 'Is the field open to more than one perhaps?'

'No…' She gave him a hardened look. 'I've so far been able to narrow it down to just the one.'

'I'm very glad to hear it. Paternity cases these days are the pits. So who is it?'

'You're not going to believe it.'

'Try me,' he said, leaning even further back in his chair, one arm slung casually over the back.

'You.'

This time he did flinch.

'*Me?*' He got to his feet, his chair flying backwards to slam into the filing cabinet behind. He stared at her across his desk. '*Me?*'

'You're fertile, aren't you?' she asked.

Xavier reached blindly for his abandoned chair and sat back down, the pen he'd been holding scuttling along the desk until it came to a halt beside his paperclip holder.

'You're joking of course.' His chest felt tight, as if someone was squeezing him from the inside.

'I wish.'

He sucked in a breath through his teeth. 'Are you sure?'

'Sure as eggs, to use an apt choice of phrase.'

'*Christ.*'

'I've already tried appealing to the higher powers but so far no good.' She sent him a reproachful glance. 'I'm still pregnant.'

He sent his chair back as he got to his feet once more. 'We'll have to get married...' He scraped a hand through his hair and turned to face her. 'We'll have to get married immediately.'

'No.'

'*No?*' He stared at her. 'What do you mean, no?'

'I don't want to marry you.'

'You have to marry me!' He almost shouted the words at her.

'I do not have to marry you to have your child.'

'But…but…' He sought desperately for a valid reason but could think of nothing on the hop.

'I'm not here for help,' she said. 'I'm here to let you know, that's all.'

'I will not consent to being a part-time parent!'

'You seem to have no compunction in assigning that task to thousands of other parents out there when you represent their bitter other halves.'

'That's different,' he insisted.

'How so?'

'You know it is,' he argued. 'I'm a lawyer, for God's sake. Do you think I'm going to allow myself to be screwed by another member of my profession?'

'I won't cause you any trouble.'

'If that was supposed to reassure me let me tell you it hasn't. You're nothing but trouble from the tip of your pretty little nose to your very dainty feet.'

'I'm sorry…' She felt a bubble of emotion clog her throat and fought it back down as best she could.

'Damn it!' he swore again.

She choked down another escaping sob with difficulty. 'I should never have agreed to have that drink with you…' She bent her head to avoid his angry glare and added brokenly, 'I just wanted you to know…'

He frowned as he looked at the calendar on his desk. 'You certainly haven't rushed the announcement.' He mentally calculated the weeks back to the conference. 'How many weeks are you now? Sixteen?'

She nodded.

His eyes shifted to her abdomen. 'Are you showing?' His voice sounded distinctly husky but she imagined it was the aftermath of his shock.

'I can't do up my top button on my skirt,' she answered miserably.

He let out another harsh breath. 'How the hell am I going to tell my family?'

Carli gaped at him. 'Is that all you can think about?' She got to her feet in agitation. 'Don't you realise what this means for me?'

He returned her glare with a look of blank bewilderment.

'I'm pregnant, for God's sake!' she said. 'I didn't ask to be or plan to be, but somehow through some trick of nature I find myself in this condition. What has your family got to do with it? What about my career?'

'You'll have to give it up temporarily.'

Her eyes flared with anger. 'And do what? Go down on bended knee in gratitude for your provision? I'd rather die!'

'You can't possibly work for the whole length of your pregnancy,' he said.

'Excuse me?' She hit him with her flashing, defiant eyes. 'Did I hear you correctly?'

His jaw tightened. 'You heard me.'

'I will not give up my job for you or anybody!'

'You can hardly work through labour.'

'I'll take a few days off.'

'What if the baby gets sick?'

She bit her lip and tried to think of a solution. 'I'll employ a nanny.'

He tilted one dark brow sceptically. 'On your wage?'

'All right,' she said crisply, folding her arms across her chest. 'You pay for the nanny.'

'I'm not paying for a nanny.'

'Why ever not? It's your child!'

'I was brought up by a nanny and swore I would never allow any child of mine to suffer the same.'

Carli's mouth fell open. He'd never told her that before. She'd always imagined his childhood had been a picnic of happy, sunny days with an adoring host of female relatives to remind him of the light he cast over them from each and every one of his bodily orifices.

'I didn't know you'd had a nanny.'

'I don't wish to discuss it.' The line of his mouth was set in an intractable line.

'What else should you tell me that you've so far neglected?' she asked.

'Nothing.' His expression instantly closed over.

'I can't work without help,' she said after another pause. 'Why don't you give up your job and be a house husband?'

'You must be joking.'

'No, I wasn't joking.'

'I was afraid you weren't.'

'What's wrong, Xavier? Don't you like the feel of the boot on the other foot?'

'I can't give up my practice. You know I can't.'

'And yet you expect...no—demand me to give up mine?'

She had him in a tight corner and Xavier was not all that sure how to get out of it. He was used to pressure. He thrived on it, but somehow this was different.

Carli was having a baby.

*His* baby.

'Come on, Carli, let's be serious here. I earn ten times your wage. Why would I give that up? It would be financial suicide.'

'Let me tell you at this point that a huge number of women out there in those suburbs you've referred to so disdainfully in the past have to face exactly this sort of choice. They have no other income and must rely on their own earning power to survive to provide for their children.'

'Pregnancy is more or less a choice these days.'

'I didn't choose it!' she said.

There was a small silence.

'Didn't you?'

Her mouth fell open in shock. '*You think I did it deliberately?*'

'A lot of women do,' he put in. 'It ensures an income for a few years, if not from the welfare system then from the man nominated as father. But as you know there are ways now of establishing just who is the father.'

She got to her feet in fury. 'I can't believe I'm hearing this!' She strode towards the door but as she reached for the door knob it seemed to melt and slip away from her. She gave it another attempt but her hands seemed to be grasping at space and she slipped in a slow folding heap to the floor...

She woke to find Xavier staring down at her with a look of such concern on his face she was tempted to think the last five years hadn't passed and they were still together.

'What happened?' She struggled to get up but he held her down with a flat hand against her shoulder.

'You blacked out.'

She blinked her eyes a couple of times to restore clarity to her blurred vision.

'I've called for an ambulance.'

'That's totally unnecessary. I'm not sick.'

'You don't look all that well to me.'

'I'm under considerable stress at the moment,' she said. 'No woman looks good with the weight of the world dragging her down.'

'You don't have to take on the weight of the world all by yourself,' he said. 'I've already offered to help you.'

'I can just imagine how. You won't mind how much it costs as long as it causes the least disturbance to your routine.'

'I have some commitments but I'm sure I can make myself available if you need me.'

'You're five years too late, buddy,' she bit out resentfully.

'Better too late than not at all.'

She wished she could argue with that but there was the sound of a trolley rattling in the hallway outside, announcing the arrival of the ambulance team.

'I don't want to go to hospital.'

'I want you checked out,' he said implacably. 'I want to reassure myself that all we're dealing with here is pregnancy.'

'Isn't pregnancy enough?' she asked.

He gave her a level look. 'It could be a whole lot worse, you know.'

'Just tell me how it could be a whole lot worse,' she asked as the trolley was wheeled into the room. 'What could possibly be worse than this?'

'You could be having twins,' he said.

She rolled her eyes and faced her nemesis in the ambulance officer who had her in his sights.

'OK, let's get this over with.' She held up her hands as if under arrest.

'Is she all right, man?' the guy asked Xavier with a frown.

Xavier twirled his finger beside his temple to indicate a state of insanity. 'She's totally nuts.'

Carli opened her mouth to deny it but a cloak of blackness beckoned once more and she gave in to it with gratefulness. She didn't have the energy to deal with Xavier in this state. All she wanted to do was sleep…

Carli woke to the sound of voices murmuring softly at the end of her hospital bed.

'Is she going to be all right?' Xavier's voice sounded distinctly strained.

A female voice answered him reassuringly, 'With a little rest and a better diet she should be fine. Her blood count showed she's a bit anaemic but the iron tablets I've prescribed for her should soon fix that.'

'How long does she have to stay in hospital?' Xavier asked.

'She can go home in the morning.'

'I'll be here first thing,' he said and Carli heard the female doctor leave the room.

'I know you're not asleep,' Xavier said, turning back to the small, stiff figure in the bed.

She sat up and brushed the hair out of her face, scowling at him darkly. 'Why are you still here?'

'Why do you think I'm here?' He frowned at her. 'You've fainted twice in my company in the space of minutes. I don't want your death on my hands—the pregnancy is bad enough.'

Carli blinked back sudden tears at his terse words. She knew the pregnancy had been a terrible shock to him but did he have to keep reminding her of how distasteful it was for him to be in this situation?

Xavier looked at her intently, his heart squeezing painfully when he saw the way her small chin wobbled as a track of tears made its way down her smooth cheek.

'Oh, God.' He came over and, sitting on the edge of her bed, gathered her against him. 'I didn't mean it like that.' He spoke into the fragrant cloud of her hair.

'How else did you mean it?' She pushed him away with a choked sob. 'You hate the fact that I'm carrying your child, I know you do.'

'I don't hate the idea at all, it's just the timing of it is a little bit strange.'

'Five years too late you mean?' she asked bitterly. 'You were quite happy to build up your stud back then; we argued about little else.'

'We're divorced, Carli, surely—'

'And we're staying divorced so don't get any ideas of playing happy families with me to get access to your child.'

He held her defiant look for a lengthy moment. 'My offer of marriage was a spur-of-the-moment knee-jerk reaction and I'm retracting it here and now,' he said. 'There will be no remarriage.'

The wind went right out of Carli's sails, leaving her emotionally stranded.

What was wrong with her?

She didn't want him back.

*Did she?*

'However, I do think you should come and live with me for the rest of the pregnancy,' he said into the tight silence. 'So I can keep an eye on you.'

'I can't possibly live with you!'

'You can't possibly live alone; you heard what the doctor just said.'

'I'll be fine in a couple of days so you don't need to play at nursemaid. I couldn't think of anything worse than being under your constant surveillance. I'd go completely mad.'

His jaw tightened at her intransigence. 'Don't make it necessary for me to resort to other means to make you do as you're told.'

She balled her hands into fists as she glared at him. 'You'd have to carry me kicking and screaming back into that house with you.'

'I've had it redecorated, so it shouldn't be so repugnant to you any more.'

'I suppose you had to redecorate it to exorcise my presence.' She gave him a churlish look.

Xavier privately marvelled at how close to the truth she actually was. It had taken months before the scent of her perfume had left his house, and yet even now he sometimes thought he could still pick up a faint trace of it in the air when he was in the house alone.

'You can have your own room,' he offered.

'Thank you *very* much,' she drawled sarcastically. 'But it won't be necessary.'

'So you'll agree to share mine?'

'No!'

'Come on, Carli, let's not argue about this. There are much bigger battles we can tussle over.'

'I don't want to be a part of your life.'

'You damn well are a part of my life and will be for the next eighteen years, so the sooner you get used to it the better.' His voice rose in frustration. 'You're not doing either of us any good by being so stubborn. Haven't you stopped once to think about the baby's needs?'

She found it hard to hold his flinty look. 'I think about it all the time.'

'You've not been looking after yourself,' he said. 'You're still too thin and pale. How can you expect to nourish a growing infant on the rabbit food you insist on eating?'

'Is there anything else you'd like to criticise about me besides my stubbornness, my figure and my diet?'

'No, everything else is just perfect.'

She searched his face for signs of mockery but instead he gave her a twisted smile.

'I'm not handling this very well, am I?' he asked. 'You never really fell for the steamroller approach before so I don't imagine you will now, but I really want to do the right thing for our child.'

He had her at her most vulnerable point and she was sure he knew it.

'I want what's best as well,' she said.

'Then you'll think about it?'

'I've thought about it and the answer's still no.'

'You're one stubborn woman.' He got to his feet and looked down at her. 'But maybe I'll be able to think of a way to make you see things my way.'

'I wouldn't waste your time,' she warned. 'There's nothing you could say that would make me come back to live with you permanently. Nothing.'

'I wasn't thinking along the lines of permanently,' he said, sweeping the air out of her emotional sails again. 'Just till the baby is born, after that we'll reassess.'

She bit her lip, sure she was going to cry again and betray herself completely.

'You and I both know few marriages make the distance,' he went on as he reached for his jacket and keys on the visitor's chair. 'Ours certainly didn't but at least this time there'll be no messy, bitter divorce at the end.' He shrugged himself into his jacket and added, 'Just think of the money we'll save on legal fees.'

'Your family would be appalled to think of you getting involved with me again,' she pointed out, 'even as a platonic house guest.'

'I think under the current circumstances it's going to be difficult to convince anyone that there's nothing going on between us.'

'There is nothing going on!' she insisted vehemently.

'Are you absolutely sure about that?'

'Of course I'm sure,' she said determinedly. 'I might be

pregnant to you but I am not having a relationship with you of any sort.'

'Not even as a friend?'

She gave him an arctic look. 'You are not high on my popularity list right now and I don't see that changing any time in the future.'

His mouth tightened a fraction. 'We can hardly co-parent a child without conducting some sort of relationship.'

'I want as little contact with you as possible.'

'Well, then,' he said as he reached for the door. 'You're going to have quite a fight on your hands, young lady. Don't say I didn't warn you.'

She tilted her chin and met his challenging glare. 'You're not going to win this, Xavier. I won't allow you to.'

He gave her an imperious smile, his eyes glinting with confidence. 'Want to lay a bet on that, Carli?'

She opened her mouth but before she could deliver her cutting response he had already gone, the door swinging shut behind him.

She flopped back on the pillows, her breath going out on a whoosh of sound.

'All right, Mr High and Mighty Xavier Knightly,' she addressed the ceiling above her head with steely determination, 'if it's a fight you want, then a fight is exactly what you're going to get.'

# CHAPTER TWO

WHEN Xavier arrived at the hospital the next day to arrange to take Carli home he was shocked and more than a little annoyed to hear his ex-wife had already left.

'Where is she?' He frowned down at the ward clerk.

'I have no idea, Mr Knightly.' The clerk gave him an assessing look. 'Maybe she doesn't want *you* to know.'

He let out one short, sharp curse which sent the woman's eyebrows even higher.

'She expressly told us not to give you her address.'

'Did she, now?'

'She did.' The clerk folded her arms and gave him a you-don't-scare-me look. 'And as you no doubt know all our patients' files are strictly confidential. Unless you are a direct relative you are not entitled to any information to do with Ms Gresham.'

'Thank you for your help,' he tossed at her sarcastically as he swung for the door.

'My pleasure, Mr Knightly.'

'Yeah, right.'

He strode out to his car and while he drove phoned his secretary. 'Elaine, get me Carli's address. Do whatever you have to do to find it.'

'Don't you have it?'

'Of course not!' he ground out. 'She's my ex-wife. The last thing I wanted after our divorce was her bloody address!'

'Why do you want it now?'

'Because I have to find her and—' He stalled and

drummed his fingers on the steering wheel. 'Will you stop with all the invasive questions and get me her address otherwise your superannuation package is going to be trimmed considerably?'

His secretary laughed. 'I'll call you back in five minutes.'

'Make it three or you're fired.'

She called him back in two and a half.

'Carli has an apartment at Epping.' She gave him the address and added, 'But I think you should calm down before you go and see her.'

'Thanks for the advice but you know where you can stick it.'

'Only trying to help.'

'Go and type some letters—isn't that what I pay you to do?' He snapped off the connection but he was sure he'd caught the tail end of another laugh all the same. 'Women,' he muttered savagely and gunned the engine once more.

He pulled up in front of the apartment block forty-five minutes later, his shirt sticking to his back in spite of the state-of-the-art air-conditioning in his car.

He knew Elaine was probably right. He had to get himself under some sort of control before he talked to Carli. She was already fragile without him coming to tear strips off her for deserting him at the hospital.

Did she hate him so much?

His stomach gave a painful clench.

Yes, she did. Why else would she disappear without telling him of her whereabouts?

He went to the front door and scanned the names on the residents' list. She was on the tenth floor and he pressed his finger to the call button.

No answer.

He ground his teeth for a moment and then pressed the

button again, this time leaving his finger on it even though the buzzing noise was grating to say the least.

'Who is it?' Carli's voice came through faintly after forty-five excruciating seconds.

'It's me.'

There was a tiny pause.

'Go away. I don't want to see you.'

'We have things to discuss. We can do it through this scratchy little intercom where all the neighbours coming past will hear us or I can come up. Your choice.'

She didn't answer for such a long time he thought she'd left the intercom off the hook. He was about to press the button once more when her voice came through again.

'I'll come down. We can go to the park to talk. I want to be on neutral ground.'

'All right, have it your way. But at least let me into the building. I feel like a stalker out here.'

The doors pinged open and he stepped through and waited in front of the lifts, staring at the numbers to see which one would carry her down to him.

He followed the right-hand lift's journey to the ground floor and as its doors sprang open he stepped forward, only to stop suddenly when an elderly lady with a shopping cart gave him the evil eye as she came shuffling out.

'Who are you?' she asked. 'How did you get in here?'

He opened his mouth to tell her when Carli's voice spoke from behind him. 'It's all right, Miss Mickleton. He is my…guest.'

Xavier swung around. 'How did you get down? Is there another lift?'

She shook her head. 'I took the stairs.'

'*Ten floors?*'

'Going down is a whole lot easier than going up.'

His mouth dropped open. '*You climb up ten flights of stairs?*'

'I didn't used to but ever since the lift jammed that night...' Her cheeks grew a delicate shade of pink. 'Besides, I like the exercise.'

'Oh, for God's sake, Carli! You can't possibly think you'll still be able to do that in a few weeks' let alone a few months' time?'

She gave him a warning look and he turned to see the elderly neighbour standing listening to every word.

He turned back to Carli and muttered in an undertone, 'Come on—let's get out of here. She's giving me the creeps.'

'I heard that, young man!' Miss Mickleton said.

'You'll hear a whole lot more if you stay around long enough,' he ground out and pressed the button to release the exit.

'You were extremely rude to her,' Carli said once they were outside, walking towards the park.

'She asked for it.'

'She's a lonely old lady with no family,' she said. 'You had no right to insult her.'

'I'm not here to discuss your neighbours and their little hang-ups, I'm here to talk about us. We have a situation to resolve. And if another woman, young, old or middle-aged, gives me a serve I won't be answerable to the consequences.'

'Great to know I'm not the only woman who gives you a hard time.' She couldn't help a tiny smile as she glanced up at his brooding expression. 'Who else has rattled your chain?'

'That prison-guard chick at the hospital for a start,' he bit out. 'And then my secretary forgot where her next pay-check is coming from by offering me advice I neither wanted nor needed, as well as asking some pretty invasive questions, so I'm afraid by the time I got to the granny at your place I was in a filthy temper. I was expecting you in the lift, not some old crow with a beaky nose and a prying eye.'

'Poor you; my heart bleeds.'

'Why did you do a runner on me anyway?' He stopped walking to look down at her.

'I didn't feel up to another argument with you. I decided it would be easier to let the dust settle for a bit till we'd both cooled down. Anyway,' she gave him a suspicious look from beneath her eyelashes, 'how did you know where to find me? I'm not listed in the phone book.'

He let out his breath and continued walking, slowing his pace to match hers. 'On the odd rare occasion my secretary demonstrates she is actually worth the amount of money I pay her.'

Carli felt another smile tugging at her mouth at his dry statement. She was beginning to think he'd finally found the perfect secretary, someone who stood up to him instead of being intimidated by his threats and stormy moods.

'How long have you lived in that apartment?' he asked after another few paces.

'I bought it with the divorce settlement,' she told him. 'I've lived here ever since.'

'Alone?'

'From time to time.'

He swung his gaze back down to hers. 'Male or female?'

'Now who's asking the invasive questions?' She gave him an ironic look.

He frowned and resumed walking in silence until they came to a small park, waiting until they'd both sat down on a bench to speak.

'Carli…' He took one of her hands and gave it a quick squeeze. 'I really want you to come and live with me.'

'No.' She removed her hand from the warmth of his.

'I promise I won't touch you.'

'I don't believe you.'

He didn't like to tell her he didn't believe himself! God, he was hard now thinking of her sitting so close with his child growing in her womb. He would have to be strong for she oozed sensuality from every inch of her body. Even the way she looked at him turned his thermostat up to boiling point.

'What's your biggest objection?' he asked. 'Is it just a general feeling or something specific?'

'How can you ask me that?' She glared at him crossly. 'We wouldn't even be in this situation if you hadn't been so *specific* in your intentions.'

'I did not mean to make love that day. I swear it.'

'Try again, Mr Knightly; the lie detector just caught you out.'

'Well…' he gave her one of his carefully rationed smiles '…I must confess when I got stuck in that lift with you I was getting a little hot and bothered.'

'You didn't show it.'

'I could hardly unzip my trousers with that security camera above our heads taping everything.'

She frowned at him, her colour suddenly high. God, she hadn't even thought about security cameras. She'd been too busy fighting her attraction to him.

'If it hadn't been for the camera I was going to suggest it in the lift as a way to kill time but kind of figured it mightn't go down so well if we landed in the basement as a result. But then on reflection, if we'd died—think of what a way to go.'

Carli felt the betraying heat pool between her thighs at

his words and, crossing her legs primly, turned her body away from the tempting warmth of his.

'So you waited until we were all alone,' she said with a touch of bitterness. 'How very considerate of you.'

'Look, it won't happen again. I know you don't believe me but I will keep my hands to myself in future.'

'You don't know how to walk past a woman without touching her.'

'I didn't touch Granny back there and I wouldn't touch the ward clerk with a sterile mop, and as for my secretary she's almost old enough to be my mother.'

'Which leaves only me.'

'I can be celibate.'

'That's like asking a lion to be a vegetarian.'

'Come on, Carli, give me a break. I don't want to miss out on seeing my baby grow inside you. I want to feel its first movements and I want to see your body go through the changes. Don't shut me out.'

She bit her lip in uncertainty.

He would miss out on an awful lot if he didn't to see her for weeks if not months on end. He was the baby's father after all. Surely he had some sort of right? In her work as a legal-aid lawyer in the poorer suburbs of Sydney, she'd dealt with enough non-custodial fathers to know how painful it was for them to only see their children fortnightly, if at all.

Besides that, her fainting spells had seriously frightened her. What if she were to fall down the stairs and injure the baby? Ten flights of stairs were hard enough now—what was she going to be like in a few more weeks? She knew she should just bite the bullet and get back in the lift as if the breakdown at the conference hotel hadn't happened but...

'Can I think about it and get back to you?' she asked, buying some time.

'I'll give you a week.'

'Two.'

'Ten days.'

She let her breath out in a sigh of defeat. 'All right, ten days. I'll give you my answer then.'

He seemed satisfied with this answer and after a short conversation on neutral topics he walked her back home.

'I'll come up in the lift with you,' he said at the door.

'No…I can manage the stairs.'

'And risk harming my child? No way. If you won't take the lift I'll carry you up.'

'All right.' She took a deep breath and approached the lift. 'I'll go up in the lift.'

'Atta girl!' He grinned as she pressed the button.

'You can leave now.' She gave him an irritated look.

'You must think I'm more of a jerk than I realised,' he observed. 'I know very well as soon as my back is turned you are going to slip out of the lift and go up the stairs. 'No.' He folded his arms across the broad expanse of his chest. 'I think I'll wait until I see all the pretty numbers up there indicating your safe arrival at your door.'

'You are really a very annoying man.' She stabbed at the button once more. 'Did I ever tell you that before?'

'Only about one thousand and ninety-odd times—once a day during the three years of our marriage—would be a good estimate, don't you agree?'

The lift opened and she stepped in. 'Go back to your cave, Xavier. You sure as hell don't belong in mine.'

The doors closed on his teasing smile but it took her all of nine and a half floors to cool down.

It was then that she realised what he'd done. He'd deliberately taken her mind off her worries about the lift and it had worked. She hadn't thought about the lift at all.

She'd thought about him instead...

Xavier stared at the appointment card that came with the morning's post a few days later.

'What's this?' he asked his secretary, who was hovering about the filing cabinet.

'It's an ultrasound appointment. Your ex-wife sent it in case you wanted to see the baby.'

He dropped the card on his desk and looked at her. 'How did you know about the baby?'

She pointed to the teddy-bear ears she could see poking out of the top of a well-known toy store carrier bag. 'Clues, Mr Knightly,' she imitated his court-room sombre tones with stunning accuracy, 'clues which are pertinent to the case.'

'I can see I'm not giving you enough work to do around here,' he scowled.

'How far along is she?'

'Four months.'

'A winter baby, then.'

'I'm not sure of the due date,' he confessed, clicking his pen absently. 'Some time in June, I imagine.'

'So the conference that you said was a complete and utter waste of time turned out to be productive after all?' Elaine gave him a cheeky grin.

He threw her a filthy look and she laughed.

'Don't worry, Xavier, I think you'll make a great father.'

'I didn't do so well as a husband; God knows how I'll mess up parenting.'

'Is it impertinent of me to ask what went wrong in your marriage?' Elaine said.

He tossed the pen aside and pushed his chair back as he

got to his feet, giving her another glowering look in the process. 'Yes, it is.'

'Have you told your family yet?'

'I'm working up the courage.'

'Good luck.'

'Yeah…' He raked his hand through his hair. 'Luck's exactly what I need right now.'

Carli looked up from the magazine she was reading in the doctor's waiting room to see Xavier approach.

'Hi.' He brushed her cheek with one finger. 'How are you?'

'Fine.' She could feel the skin of her cheek still tingling from his touch long after he had sat down beside her, his long legs stretched out in front of him almost cutting the waiting room in half.

She stared across at his legs so close to hers and couldn't stop an inward shiver of reaction as she recalled how it had felt to have them between hers, his hard male body exploding with release in that fiery moment when all control had broken loose.

The trouble was she had no self-control where Xavier was concerned.

He'd been her first and only lover, taking her to bed on their second date without a single protest from her in spite of all her mother had taught her about the untrustworthy physical motives of men. She'd fallen for him almost as soon as she'd met him at her friend Eliza's wedding. He had been the best man and she had been the bridesmaid, and from the very first moment they were introduced, sparks of attraction had crackled like electricity volts charging along a metal wire. She'd seen his dark blue eyes begin to undress her on the spot and her spine had begun to tingle with anticipation. She'd boldly returned his look, doing her own bit of undressing until the heat coming her way had threatened to consume her right there on the spot. When he'd kissed her in the reception-centre car park later that evening her senses had gone into overload. Nothing in her limited experience had prepared her for the commanding pressure of his arrogantly possessive kiss, the bold, searching thrust of his tongue, or the sensuous slide of his hands as they shaped her and brought her to the hard ridge of his desire pulsing between his legs…

'Thanks for asking me to come,' Xavier said, turning in his seat to look at her.

For a moment Carli was completely thrown. She stared at him, her cheeks already heating up from the inside, and she seriously wondered if he'd been able to read her mind.

'Th…thanks for—er—coming,' she said, shifting her gaze.

Out of the corner of her eye she saw him check his watch before he reached to pick up a magazine off the table beside him.

'I'm sorry I'm a bit late,' he said, turning a page. 'I had a meeting with a client that went over time.'

'Difficult case?' she asked, chancing a glance his way.

He seemed to pause before he answered, his eyes going back to the magazine he was holding in his hands. 'Small kids and a couple of properties. It's going to get dirty, I can tell.'

'Whose side are you on, the wife's or the husband's?'

Again he seemed to hesitate, the rustle of the pages being turned seeming to make the silence stretch even further before he answered, 'The husband's.'

She turned back to her own magazine. 'I'm sure you'll do what's best for all involved.'

Xavier recognised the element in her tone which suggested she thought no such thing and deep down he couldn't help feeling annoyed by it. Her bitterness towards him ran deep and he knew once she found out about the Dangars' divorce it would only make things a whole lot worse.

'I always try to be fair.'

She closed the magazine and looked at him again. 'Would you be so fair if it was the wife you were representing?'

'If I thought it was appropriate. Sometimes ex-wives can be brutal in their demands. I do what I can to redress the balance but it doesn't always work out to everyone's satisfaction.'

Carli was saved the necessity of a reply as her name was called.

'Carla Gresham?'

She got to her feet and privately wondered how long it had been since she'd thought of herself as the sophisticated Carla.

Had she ceased to exist?

Was Carli back?

The Carli who loved Xavier with all the strength of her being?

The vulnerable Carli who'd been so hurt five years ago and still hadn't quite yet recovered...

The doctor explained the procedure to them both and once Carli was positioned on the table she spread some conductor gel over the slight mound of her belly and began rolling the probe back and forth while looking at the monitor beside the table.

'Do you want to know the sex?' Dr Green asked, looking at the screen.

'Yes.'

'No.'

Xavier backed down. 'All right—no.'

The doctor turned and smiled. 'It's not always one hundred per cent certain at this stage; I've been known to get it wrong, but not often. But if you like surprises it's nice to wait until the day of birth.'

She moved the probe a few more times and showed them the tiny heart beat and the curve of the developing spine, the tiny hands and feet and the head which seemed too big for the little body.

'All is as it should be at this stage,' Dr Green assured them. 'How are the iron tablets going?'

'I haven't fainted since those first couple of times.'

'Good.' She pressed the print-out button and handed them each a copy. 'I'll see you again in a few weeks but in the meantime take care of yourself. My receptionist will arrange a time for you and give you some details of a parenting class you can attend if you are interested.'

While Carli was receiving her next appointment date, Xavier found himself staring down at the photograph in his hands. He could hardly believe what he was seeing was true. The tiny figure was his child, now in the second trimester of development. The child he had longed for five years ago to repair their crumbling marriage. How ironic that his baby was conceived well after the demise of their relationship! His heart swelled with emotion at the thought of holding his offspring moments after birth, of watching him or her grow into toddlerhood then on to childhood, the first day of school…

He pulled himself up short with a reminder of the current state of his relationship with Carli. It was still a war zone and there was no sign of peace in sight, but maybe if he tried really hard he'd be able to bring her round.

Damn it! He *had* to bring her round!

Carli tucked the appointment card in her purse and followed Xavier outside to where her car was parked.

'Can we have dinner tonight?' he asked as she unlocked the door.

Her hand stalled on the door handle. 'I don't think...'

'I'll pick you up at seven.'

'I don't get home from work till half past.'

'Why ever not?' he asked.

'I've already taken the morning off. I have to catch up on some paperwork as well as deal with my usual appointments.'

'Call in sick.'

'But I'm not sick.'

'Pretend just this once.'

'No. I don't think it's fair to my clients. I have a full list of them this afternoon and I couldn't cancel even if I wanted to.'

'Which of course you wouldn't,' he bit out, unable to hide his frustration any longer, 'because even though you are now expecting my child you don't want to have anything to do with me—isn't that right?'

She gave him a hard look and wrenched open her door. 'Got it in one, Mr Knightly.'

'I won't take no for an answer,' he warned her. 'I think you know me well enough to be assured of that.'

He stepped back as she slammed the door closed, the spluttering of her engine as she started the car for some reason making him even more irritated as if it too were giving him the brush-off.

He stood and watched her drive off, toying with the idea of following her and making her change her mind, but only last week the ex-wife of one of his clients had slapped an

AVO on his client for similar behaviour and he knew Carli would have no hesitation in doing the same to him, and probably do it a whole lot quicker too.

He wasn't used to feeling so out of control in a situation. Even during their break-up he'd always maintained the upper hand, even though his conscience had troubled him for months afterwards at the way he'd handled things.

His reputation as a brutal legal eagle had spilled over into his personal life, making him appear ruthless and clinically unfeeling when in fact nothing could be further from the truth.

He still had feelings for Carli but he wasn't entirely sure what they were. For years he'd squashed any thought of her as he'd found it so painful. He desired her but then a lot of ex-husbands somehow viewed their previous wives in a possessive sense in spite of a bitter divorce.

Was he such a man? Unable to let go? Unable to allow her the same freedom he now took for granted?

He'd had several lovers in the past five years, none of them particularly serious, but the thought of Carli with someone else was…he clenched his fists against the tide of jealousy that almost swamped him.

He couldn't bear the thought of some other man in her life. It nauseated him to think of her arms wrapped around someone else's neck, her soft, panting cries of pleasure in someone's else's ear, her sweat-slicked body in someone else's arms.

He wanted her back.

Simple as that.

He wanted her back.

On any terms…even if he had to engineer some to get his way.

*   *   *

Carli's last client of the day had not long left when a call came through from one of her old but now distant friends, Elizabeth Dangar.

'Eliza…' She searched her brain for a valid excuse for not having made contact for so long. She had longed to, but because of Aidan's close relationship with Xavier she'd avoided socialising with her ever since the divorce, even to the point of missing both of her children's christenings in case she inadvertently ran into Xavier. 'I've been meaning to call you…I've been busy and—'

'Carli…' There was the sound of a choked sob. 'I have to talk to you. Are you with someone right now?'

'No, my last client just left. Whatever's the matter? Are the kids all right?'

'Aidan wants a divorce.'

Carli almost dropped the phone in shock. Elizabeth and Aidan Dangar were quite possibly the only couple she'd thought would stay together forever. Their love had seemed so genuine, so intense…but then hadn't hers for Xavier?

'I don't know what to say… Are you OK? I mean, what will you do? Are you getting custody of Amelia and Brody?'

'I haven't got a chance,' Eliza sobbed.

'Why ever not?' Carli's hand on the phone tightened. 'Brody's only ten months old, for God's sake! Surely Aidan wouldn't do that! And Amelia's just about to start school. There isn't a family-court lawyer this side of Bourke who would agree to take your kids off you permanently.'

'You don't think so?' Eliza asked between sobs. 'What about that ex-husband of yours? He's exactly the sort of lawyer who would do it.'

Carli felt the spider-like legs of trepidation creep all over the surface of her skin, lingering the longest amongst the sensitive hairs on the back of her neck.

'Xavier's acting for Aidan?' she asked in a choked gasp.

'Of course he is,' Eliza said bitterly. 'They went to the same private academy and you know all about that old school-tie thing. Xavier Knightly will relish in destroying me, especially as he knows you and I have been friends for so long.'

As much as Carli hated to admit it, Eliza's point was painfully valid.

'You've got to speak to him, Carli. You've got to speak to him to tell him to change his mind.'

'Who?' Carli asked. 'Aidan?'

'No,' Eliza said. 'You have to speak to Xavier. I know you haven't seen him in years but surely just this once you could see him and plead with him not to take on this case?'

Carli wondered what her friend would say if she told her she'd already seen him and got herself pregnant to him in the process.

'You're my only hope, Carli,' Eliza cried before she could answer. 'I can't afford the sort of legal fees I'd need to pay to fight this and I don't qualify for legal aid.'

'I could represent you,' Carli said with reckless impulsivity, 'pro bono, of course.'

'You'd do that?' Eliza asked. 'You'd take on the toughest legal eagle in town?'

'I don't see why not.'

'But you were married to him for three years!'

'What's that got to do with it? I'm a lawyer, so is he.'

'No offence, Carli, but he'll eat you alive. I can't let you do it. In fact, I forbid you to. You were so broken up after your divorce; can you imagine what it would do to you to face him in a family law court?'

Carli knew it was hardly the time to inform her friend she'd recently faced him under much more intimate conditions, but it wouldn't be too long before she had to. Her pregnancy was already starting to show and if she was to meet Eliza face to face in the not so distant future she knew her friend would see for herself that one and one had very definitely made three.

'Look.' She gave her fingertips a quick drum on the desk top. 'I'll tell you what I'll do. I'll arrange to have dinner with Xavier and try and talk him out of representing Aidan. Who knows? I might be able to persuade him to hand him over to a more junior client in the firm. In the meantime, I'll put my ear to the ground to find someone to act for you who won't baulk at facing Xavier and who also hopefully won't charge the sort of fees that puts Ferraris in most lawyer's garages.'

'You're an angel, Carli. I knew I could rely on you. Call me as soon as you can, OK?'

'I'll do that, but in the interim have you considered some counselling?'

'Aidan would never agree to that!'

'What about for you?' Carli suggested. 'It can be tremendously helpful to have someone neutral to discuss issues with.'

'You think I'm crazy or something?' Eliza's tone had hardened. 'I'm not some sort of crackpot who needs to see a shrink.'

Carli frowned at the defensiveness in her friend's tone. 'Honey, I didn't for a moment suggest that. Look, I had counselling myself and—'

'Yeah, but it didn't stop you getting a divorce, did it?'

'There are counsellors and there are *counsellors*,' Carli said, wishing she'd thought to shop around a bit more herself five years ago. 'But even if the divorce still goes ahead at least you will know you gave it your best shot.'

There was the sound of a small child crying in the

background and Carli knew the conversation was more or less over.

'I've got to go,' Eliza said. 'Will you call me and let me know how things go with Xavier?'

'Sure I will; now stop worrying and take each day as it comes. I'll come and see you as soon as I can, all right?'

'Thanks,' Eliza said. 'Good luck.'

'Yeah right,' Carli said as the connection ended with a click. 'I'm going to need more than luck.'

She sat and nibbled on the end of a ragged nail for a minute, her thoughts flying around her head like a flock of startled pigeons.

Before she allowed herself a chance to change her mind she reached for the telephone again and dialled Xavier's office number.

He picked it up on the first ring and answered gruffly, 'Xavier Knightly.'

'Have you fired your secretary?' she asked without announcing herself.

She heard the creak of leather as he sat back in his chair. 'I'm seriously considering it, but no—I haven't as yet. Besides, it's close to seven-thirty; she doesn't do overtime.' The leather gave another protest as he asked, 'What can I do for you? Have you changed your mind about dinner?'

'I have actually.'

'Oh?' She heard his pen click. 'What brought that on?'

'Hunger.'

'You must be starving if you've consented to spending the evening with me.'

'Ravenous.'

'Good. I'll be there in half an hour, subject to traffic, of course.'

'I'm not at home yet,' she said. 'I'm still at the office.'

'Shall I fetch you from there?'

'No, I need to get changed. I'll meet you at my apartment in about forty-five minutes, OK?'

'I'll wait outside,' he said. 'I don't want to come across the wicked witch from the north-west again.'

'Don't tell me you're frightened of a little old lady, Xavier?'

'No.' His tone was wry. 'It's the young and beautiful pregnant ones that spook me most. See you in forty.'

'Forty-five.'

'Thirty-five and the clock is already ticking.' He put the phone down before she could answer and got to his feet with a punch of victory into the air.

'*Yes!*'

# CHAPTER THREE

CARLI had only just changed into a loose-fitting dress when the intercom sounded announcing Xavier's arrival downstairs.

She did her best to ignore the fluttery sensation in her stomach as she quickly applied a fresh coat of lip gloss to her mouth, but her hand shook all the same.

She told him through the intercom she'd be down in a minute and, taking one last reassuring glance in the mirror, made her way down the stairs.

He was standing outside dressed in charcoal-grey trousers and an open white shirt, his tall, handsome figure sending the air right out of Carli's lungs as soon as her eyes came to rest on him. She wondered if there would be a time in the future when he would cease to have such an effect on her, or would she always experience this shock-wave of feeling whenever he was within touching distance?

He gave her a reproving look as she came through the security door. 'Are you still taking the stairs?'

'Every gym from Bondi to Blacktown has a stair-climber,' she argued. 'I'm saving myself a fortune in membership fees by using the stairs.'

'What you're doing is risking our baby's health, that's what you're doing.'

Carli frowned at the disapproval in his voice. 'I'm doing no such thing! Exercise is very good for pregnant women. It helps to regulate weight and strengthen the body for labour.'

'Why not swim instead?'

She rolled her eyes. 'Look, Xavier, I work a twelve-hour day as it is. Where the hell would I find time to stop off at a pool and do a few laps?'

'I have a pool,' he said. 'Remember?'

She tore her eyes away from the provocative glint in his gaze as a host of erotic memories flooded her brain of all the times in the past when the swimming-pool water had almost boiled with the heat of their passion.

'What sort of food do you fancy?'

His swift change of subject threw her momentarily. 'I don't mind—you choose.'

He gave her a wry look as he helped her into the car. 'You're seriously scaring me with this sudden submissive-female routine. It's totally out of character.'

'I truly don't mind what we eat,' she said, ignoring his penetrating gaze.

He pursed his lips for a moment as if in deep thought. 'OK, let's get it over with. What's on your mind?'

'Nothing.'

'Yes, there is.'

'I'm hungry so why don't we have dinner? If you re- member, you were the one who issued the invitation in the first place.'

He closed her door and came around to the driver's seat, waiting until they were on their way before he spoke again.

'Have you given any more thought to my offer?'

'I have four more days to decide,' she reminded him.

'I know, but I'd like a progress report.'

She gnawed at her lip gloss for a moment. 'Can we dis- cuss it some other time?'

He glanced her way. 'Why not now?'

'Because I don't want to argue with you while you're driving.'

'Which means your answer's still no,' he surmised.

'What did you expect me to do?' She gave him a frowning look. 'Throw all my stuff in my car and drive straight over?'

'There was a time when you would've done exactly that.'

'That was a long time ago, Xavier, and I'm no longer a naïve young girl. There are quite a lot of things I wouldn't do if I had my time over again.'

'Want to be a little more specific?' His tone hardened. 'Why don't you come right out and say it? I can take it. I know you regret our time together.'

'It wasn't exactly a picnic from day one,' she pointed out coldly.

'I was building my career; you know how hard it is to juggle everything else as well. I did my best, Carli, but too late realised it wasn't good enough for your exacting standards.'

'My exacting standards?' She let out a choked gasp of affront. 'You were the one with the check-list of what you wanted in a wife. No career, no ambition, no brain.'

'That's not true and you damn well know it. I didn't mind you having a career, it's just that—'

'You have no idea of the struggles normal people face to get their careers up and running,' she cut him off. 'You walked into your father's office and took over, for God's sake! How hard was that?'

'Nepotism had nothing to do with it! I had to be interviewed along with every other applicant.'

'Were any of the other applicants female?' she asked.

There was a slight pause as he swerved around a driver trying to park.

'No, I don't think so.'

'Of course there wouldn't have been. The firm of Knightly and Knightly and Associates is known for its deeply entrenched misogyny—no woman in her right mind

would have even applied. The glass ceiling is doubly re-
inforced and totally shatterproof. No one can see up and
those at the top have absolutely no interest in seeing down.'

'I hardly see that it's my fault the majority of my father's
colleagues and mine are male. My grandfather started the
firm and my father and I have simply followed in his footsteps.'

'But that's the whole point!' Carli railed. 'You can't see
the privileged position you occupy because you're male and
have never had to fight to be treated equally.'

'Can we please change the subject?' He changed gears
with unnecessary force. 'I don't want to be drawn into yet
another one of your feminist arguments which will no doubt
end up with me crossing my legs all evening in case you're
tempted to take a swipe.'

'You are being so typically male and obstructive. I can't
believe a man with three sisters can be so unenlightened.'

'Look, Carli—I love women, you know that. I have nothing against equal pay and all that but let's face it, women
still have babies and the period during which childbirth is
ideal for women unfortunately coincides with the time of a
major career push. There's really no way around it. Most
women eventually have to make a choice between children
and a high-powered career; it's just too hard to have both.'

'That's only because men refuse to change. I read a study
recently which cited the appalling statistics on male con-
tribution to household tasks; that is, of course, if the male
is still around. Most women are left holding the babies and
the washing, the ironing, the shopping, the cooking, the—'

'OK, OK.' He held up a hand to stall her diatribe. 'I take
your point. I know not every man is perfect when it comes
to housework.'

'Someone from your privileged background may not
realise this but a lot of women out there in the suburbs hold

down full-time jobs as well as care for a family. They have no spare time and no spare cash for housekeepers and gardeners and cooks. That's the real world out there, Xavier.' She pointed to the sea of red roofs they had driven past. 'And it isn't always pretty.'

'You make it sound as if I've been totally cloistered all my life,' he said.

'You have. You've been sheltered from reality by wealth and privilege. Your mother never worked outside the home and nor did she work within it if that bevy of household staff had anything to do with it.'

'What about your parents?' he asked. 'You've never told me much about them. Did they both work?'

'You know I don't like discussing them.'

He frowned as he pulled up in front of the restaurant he'd selected and, once he stopped the car, turned to look her way. 'Methinks therein lies a clue.'

She turned away from his contemplative look and opened the door to avoid giving a response.

He locked the car and came to where she was waiting on the pavement and gently took her arm. He gave her a twisted smile as he looked down at her. 'Time for a change of subject?'

She felt a tiny reluctant smile tug at her mouth and nodded. 'Arguing with you is so exhausting. I never realised how much so until now.'

'Only because you're out of practice,' he said, leading her to the entrance. 'But you'll soon brush up on your skills, I'm sure.'

She followed him into the restaurant and, once they were both seated with a drink, she decided to get straight to the point of the evening.

'I wanted to talk to you about something…' She began

to absently toy with the rim of her water glass with the tip of one finger.

Xavier took a sip of his brandy and dry. 'Fire away.'

She pushed her glass aside and faced him. 'Are you currently acting for Aidan Dangar in his application for divorce from Eliza?'

He took another sip of his drink before answering. 'I don't usually discuss my clients outside of the office.'

'For God's sake, Xavier!' She was losing her patience fast. 'He's one of your closest friends.'

'I have lots of friends.' He twirled his glass.

His evasive manner annoyed her into retorting, 'I can't imagine how you hold on to them. You must be paying them for the privilege of your esteemed company.'

He put his glass down onto the table with such exaggerated precision that it delivered the same warning reflected in his dark blue gaze as it held hers.

'Careful, Carli, you don't want to make a scene in the middle of a crowded restaurant, do you?'

She fought her temper back down with difficulty, reminding herself this was about Eliza and her little children, not her.

'I know you're acting for Aidan so there's no point denying it.'

'Is that going to be a problem for you?' he asked.

'Eliza's my friend.'

'So?'

Carli stiffened at the clinical detachment in his tone. 'So I don't want you to represent Aidan. I want you to hand him over to someone else in the firm, someone more junior.'

He leant back in his chair and surveyed her face for endless seconds. 'Now, why would you want me to do that?'

She moistened her lips with her tongue before responding. 'I don't think you can maintain professional objectivity, that's why.'

'I've acted for friends and acquaintances before,' he said evenly. 'I haven't had any complaints so far.'

'That's exactly my point!' she returned. 'You'll destroy Eliza Dangar just to get back at me.'

He gave her another long studied look. 'What's it worth to you if I drop the case?'

Carli felt the slow crawl of realisation make its way through her body, making her feel as if ice instead of blood had entered her system.

He gave her one of his lazy smiles. 'How much, Carli— enough to come and live with me again?'

Her fingers around her glass tightened. 'That's blackmail.'

He gave an indolent shrug and lifted his glass back to his still smiling mouth. 'Take it or leave it. I'll hand him over if you come and live with me for the rest of your pregnancy.'

She swallowed against the restriction in her throat. 'I can't.'

'Poor Eliza,' he drawled as he twirled his glass. It was low of him, he knew, but it was a means to an end he very much desired. He had considered trying a softer approach with her but he could see she was too angry and embittered to respond to him on that level.

No, ruthless and calculating was the only way to go.

He gave her a sardonic look and mused, 'I wonder how she'll cope without full custody of the kids?'

'You bastard!' she spat at him. 'You really mean it, don't you? How can you live with yourself, playing with people's lives like that?'

'The law is the law,' he said with the same clinical detachment he'd used earlier. 'Eliza Dangar has been bordering on the psychotic for months. Did she happen to mention it to you? No, I didn't think so. It wouldn't be too hard to convince the judge of her inability to parent full-time.'

She sucked in a painful breath. 'I can't believe what I'm hearing…I didn't think even you would stoop as low as this.'

'I didn't get my reputation on hearsay, Carli. Perhaps you should remember that.'

'She's a young mother!' she said. 'She's vulnerable and—'

'She's also an unfit mother,' he interrupted. 'Aidan has been worried about issues of safety with the children. Maybe you should have spent a little more time looking into the details of the case instead of jumping straight in to castrate the nearest male in sight. Where's that professional objectivity you were harking on about?'

'You are such a jerk.'

'So you've told me.'

'I can't believe I'm sitting here with you. I should have known you'd twist things around to get your own way.'

'Is this why you agreed to have dinner with me?' he asked. 'So you could butter me up to convince me to let this case go to someone else?'

She felt the guilty colour storm into her cheeks. 'No…'

'Don't lie to me, Carli. I can see what you've been up to but it won't wash with me. I'm calling the shots here and I'm telling you unless you agree to live with me for the rest of your pregnancy your friend is going to lose her kids. Do you really want their tears on your hands?'

She was trapped.

Trapped by her very own set-up; a set-up which he had cleverly turned upside down to force her hand.

'I could report you for this,' she said through tight lips.

'Ah, but would they believe you?' he taunted her ruthlessly. 'I'm one of Sydney's highest-earning lawyers and, since you happen to be my ex-wife, what do you think the tribunal will make of that?' His dark eyes glinted with anticipatory victory. 'No, I think you'll soon see the way the pathway goes.'

'I will not resume a physical relationship with you.'

'Did I ask you to?' He leant back in his chair with languid grace.

'You're not in the habit of asking. You just do what you damn well like and to hell with the consequences.'

'Now, now, Carli, that's hardly fair; I'm the one trying to help you with the current circumstances. It wouldn't do to go snapping at the hand that in the end could very well be feeding you.'

'I'd rather die of hunger than accept anything from you.'

It was unfortunate that at that precise moment their entrées arrived. Carli looked down at the deliciously fragrant laksa she'd so looked forward to and wondered if she'd been a little too vehement.

'Eat up, Carli.' A knowing smile played about his mouth as he picked up his cutlery. 'Who knows? I might even let you foot the bill.'

She picked up her spoon and wished she had the courage to throw it at his face, but her hunger got the better of her and she dipped it into the steaming coconut-milk broth instead. She silently seethed as she mechanically transferred the food to her mouth, her brain desperately trying to think of a way out of the net that was closing around her. Living with Xavier for months on end was just asking for trouble.

Big trouble.

She hadn't been able to resist him for that one night at the conference, how in the world was she going to keep him at arm's length while they shared his house? Living with anyone forced certain intimacies on the parties concerned. What sort of intimacies would Xavier force on her?

She could see it now, the subtle slide of her independence into grasping, needy dependence just like before. She would be hanging about waiting for him to return, grateful for a few minutes of his attention whenever he could fit her into his busy work and social schedule.

She pushed her plate away, her appetite suddenly disappearing.

'Is something wrong with your entrée?' Xavier asked.

'I've had enough.'

He frowned as he inspected the contents of her bowl. 'You've barely touched it. Is it too hot and spicy for you?'

The only thing too hot and spicy for her was him but she could hardly tell him that!

'I hope you're not going to stand over me every time we share a meal,' she said instead, her gaze caustic as it connected with his.

'If I have to force-feed you then I will add it to my list of daily duties,' he answered evenly. 'Now, won't that be fun? Food fights…mmm. Do you remember that time with the whipped cream?'

Carli felt her face heating up and reached for a bread roll to distract herself from his taunting look. She tore it apart savagely, lavishly spreading it with butter and stuffing bits of it into her mouth to stop herself from engaging in conversation with him.

Xavier chuckled as he handed her another bread roll once that one was finished. 'Do you want me to order some more?'

'I want you to shut the hell up,' she said, pushing the bread roll away.

He leant back in his seat and surveyed her flustered features for a lengthy moment.

'You don't like thinking about what we had together, do you?' he asked.

She was saved from having to respond when the waiter appeared to clear their entrées away. She didn't want to remember the good times. It hurt too much.

Once the waiter was gone Xavier redirected the conversation. 'How much longer do you expect to stay at work?'

'I intend to keep working as long as possible.'

'Don't you think you might need some time to get used to the idea of motherhood?' he asked. 'Maybe you should have a few weeks off before the birth to prepare yourself.'

'Do you realise that indigenous women in past times simply squatted and delivered and then carried on with the rest of the tribe?' she said with considerable asperity.

'Yes, I do happen to know that and I also know the infant and maternal fatality rate of that time. This is the twenty-first century, Carli—people do not squat and deliver any more, or at least not in the middle of Sydney.'

She held his challenging look for as long as she could but in the end she had to lower her gaze first.

'I haven't had time to think about all the details,' she said. 'I don't even know how I'll cope as a mother.' A vision of her worn-out mother flitted into her brain, making her stomach hollow in fear. Would she too end up like that? And wasn't she already halfway there with her uncontrollable need of a man who no longer loved her?

'You'll be fine when the time comes,' Xavier assured her as he topped up her glass of water.

'I wish I had your confidence.'

'I'll be there to help you,' he reminded her.

She crushed her napkin in her lap and lifted her eyes back to his. 'Have you told your family about…us?'

He reached for his glass and took a small sip before

answering, 'I was thinking of paying them a visit some time later this week.'

'Don't you mean deliver them a *fait accompli?*'

He gave a shrug of one broad shoulder. 'What I do is my business. If I choose to get involved with my ex-wife once more surely that's my affair?'

'It was hardly a choice,' she said. 'If I wasn't pregnant we wouldn't be sitting here now, would we?'

His eyes held hers for a long moment. 'Maybe not, but I have a feeling we might have been somewhere else much more comfortable.'

Her brows drew together in a frown. 'What are you saying?'

'I'm saying it's not over. What we had hasn't died in spite of our divorce.'

'What you're talking about is merely the most fundamental physical attraction. We'll get over it in time.'

'How much time?' he asked. 'You have only to look at me in a certain way and I'm ready to burst. Five years has done nothing to dampen my desire for you.'

She bent her head to stare at a tiny spot of green-tinged laksa broth on the tablecloth rather than face the intensity of his dark blue gaze.

'Physical desire is not a good basis for a relationship,' she said. 'It will eventually burn itself out.'

'Deny it if you want but I know what I feel. I also know you feel it too otherwise we wouldn't be sitting here with a baby growing between us.'

Carli felt her breath trip in her throat. He made it sound so intimate…their bodies somehow permanently connected now their child was developing in her womb. But he hadn't mentioned caring for her, only physical desire. Would it be enough to carry them through?

'I'll organise for your apartment to be rented out,' he cut

across her private rumination. 'Someone will collect your things tomorrow. After work come straight to my house, you won't need to worry about anything for it will all be done. I don't want you packing and lifting anything in your condition.'

'Xavier...I don't think—'

'As for the Dangar case, I'll pass it on to one of the younger partners to deal with.'

She let out her breath on a sigh. 'I know I'm going to regret this. I can just feel it.'

'Stop worrying, Carli,' he said. 'We've lived together before. We're not total strangers and we have interests in common. The next few months will fly past and maybe at the end we'll be part of that rare breed of divorced couples who actually manage to become good friends.'

The rest of the meal continued with Xavier making every effort to keep the topic of conversation on neutral ground but all the time Carli felt as if she was being led further and further into more dangerous territory.

Part of her wished she had the courage to call his bluff, to simply walk away and let him do his worst with the Dangars, but when she recalled the desperation in her friend Eliza's voice she knew she couldn't pull out now even if she'd wanted to.

And she didn't want to.

She stiffened in her chair as she realised what she'd finally admitted. She *wanted* to live with him, She wanted to see him each day, hear him talk, see him smile, hear him laugh, see him frown. She wanted to smell his aftershave in the air and on her clothes not to mention lingering on her skin the way it had used to do in the past. She wanted him to feel for the bulge of his child with his open palm on her growing belly, she wanted him to press her down as he brought his mouth to hers...

Xavier tossed the dessert menu aside and met her eyes across the table.

'I must say, for a woman who always swore she'd never have children you seem to have taken all of this very well.'

'What do you mean by that?' Caught off guard, Carli knew her tone sounded far too edgy and defensive. 'You still think I planned this to happen?'

He had the grace to look a little shamefaced and when he spoke his tone was distinctly gruff. 'No, of course not. I was way out of line that day. I wasn't thinking all that clearly.'

'If you think you were shocked, can you imagine what I felt when I saw the results of the test?' she said.

Xavier had thought about very little else over the last few days, wondering how she'd coped on her own for all those weeks, gradually summoning up enough courage to tell him.

God, she might never have told him.

His gut twisted painfully as he thought about his child growing up without a father.

'Children put such a strain on relationships,' she said. 'How many marriages break up once kids come on the scene?'

He returned her direct look. 'But we'll be one step ahead, Carli. We're not married any more so maybe our child will do the very opposite.'

'You mean repair the damage of our past?' She stared at him incredulously.

He gave a noncommittal shrug. 'It can happen.'

'So can miracles but they're still incredibly rare.'

He reached for the remains of his drink and tossed back the contents of the glass before speaking. 'Love and marriage didn't work for us, Carli, so I think we should concentrate on the things that do work.'

'How can this possibly work?' she asked. 'You're forcing me to do something I don't want to do.' *Liar*, her conscience whispered in her ear. You *do* want to.

'The trouble with you is half the time you don't know what it is you want. You're stuck in a going-nowhere job, you live in a poky little apartment and your car looks like it needs a serious make-over. As far as I can tell, you have little social life unless you count the odd conversation with that nosy little crone who lives in your block. For God's sake, Carli, you're young and attractive, don't throw your life away.'

'Wouldn't I be throwing my life away by living with you?' Her tone contained a heavy dose of irony.

'No. I won't let that happen a second time. You have my word.'

Carli wished she could believe him. She knew his observations were partially right; she had very little in the way of social life and the demands of her job were testing at times with little monetary reward for her efforts.

Over the last five years she'd become stuck in a rut, unable to go back and unable to go forward. Her break-up with Xavier had totally destroyed her confidence. She had taken the first job that came along and in spite of her misgivings had stuck at it, too afraid to move forwards to something more satisfying. She'd been marking time professionally and personally and she knew if she didn't do something soon things would never change. But how would living with Xavier solve anything? She'd been totally swamped by his career demands before, so how would it be the second time around with a baby to complicate things even further?

And then there was the matter of her feelings towards him.

She still loved him.

Couldn't in fact remember a time when she hadn't, even in the last five bitter years apart. Every time she'd thought of him her heart had squeezed with the pain of longing and regret. How much easier all this would be if he too felt the same!

She forced herself to meet his watchful gaze across the table, her hands tightening into a knot beneath the screen of the table. 'It seems I have no choice in this,' she muttered darkly.

'I wouldn't say that,' he returned, leaning back casually in his chair. 'I'm giving you the choice of living with me and having the best of health care and support for the rest of your pregnancy, or watching your friend go through a very nasty divorce.'

'You'd really do it, wouldn't you?' She glared at him. 'You'd do it just to get what you want. You hate me that much.'

He held her glare for much longer than she was comfortable with, his dark blue eyes totally inscrutable. 'Don't you think it's high time we put our issues aside and concentrated on the baby?' he asked. 'We have a lot to discuss, such as names and future schooling and so on. Personally I'd prefer to keep away from the bad things in our past; revisiting them time and time again can't change anything now.'

She dipped her spoon into her chocolate mousse with an inward sigh. He was right yet again—nothing could be changed; what they'd had previously was well and truly over. Their past had been built on love and even that had crumbled. What would their future, now built on hate and bitterness, bring forth?

In spite of her misgivings, Carli drove straight to Xavier's house in Mosman after work the next day. The traffic was slow all the way, but close to the Pacific Highway junction a minor accident had caused further mayhem.

She sat tapping her fingers on the steering wheel as the traffic lights changed four times without a single vehicle moving through the intersection. The traffic fumes made her head ache and the nausea which had been grumbling on and off all day returned with a vengeance in the close atmosphere of the car. She thought longingly of Xavier's efficient air-conditioning and fanned her face with a draft copy of a client's will, vowing she'd get her system re-gassed the next day as she'd been meaning to do for weeks.

Finally the slow crawl through the intersection began and within another thirty minutes she pulled into the driveway of her previous marital home, a host of memories assailing her as she did so.

Xavier's top-of-the-range BMW was in the open three-car garage, which she knew without looking down at her watch meant she was incredibly late. She couldn't remember a time when she'd been home after him in the whole time they'd been married and wondered if he would be annoyed with her as she had been with him in the past. She couldn't help a tiny inward cringe at how she'd behaved way back then. She had been so insistent on being treated equally she'd overlooked some of the realities of newly married life, that like any other relationship sometimes adjustments had to be made. She hadn't wanted to give an inch, terrified she would end up downtrodden and desperate like her mother, her life ceasing to function without a man to prop her up. How many times had this front door been slammed in fury as she'd stormed out on one of their heated exchanges?

It felt strange to approach it now without a key in her hand. She pressed the bell and waited for him to answer, the nerves in her stomach doing a fluttery sort of dance as she heard the firm tread of his footsteps approaching.

'Traffic bad?' he greeted her with an empathetic look, taking in her flustered appearance.

She nodded and stepped into the house as he held the door open. 'You wouldn't believe how dreadful it was.'

'I'd believe it.' He shut the door and took her briefcase. 'I just ploughed through it myself.'

She brushed the heavy hair off her neck and grimaced as another stab of pain hit her between the eyes.

'Is something wrong?' he asked, looking at her intently.

'Just a headache,' she said, dropping her handbag at her feet and rolling her shoulders for a moment. 'It's nothing to worry about.'

'Can I get you something?'

She shook her head then wished she hadn't as a fresh wave of pain squeezed at her temples. 'No, I think I'll have a shower and go straight to bed.'

'You look pale. You're not going to pass out on me, are you?' He took her wrist in one of his hands, his long fingers curling around her slender bones, his thumb on her already leaping pulse.

'No…' She pulled out of his loose hold to maintain her distance.

'Carli…' He cleared his throat and began again. 'I was thinking we could visit my parents tomorrow evening.'

'Why,' she asked, 'so you can show them my bump and tell them there's no escaping the fact that you are responsible? Mind you, I'm surprised you haven't insisted on a paternity test to make absolutely sure.' She gave him a cynical look. 'I'm sure your parents are going to insist on one.'

'I did consider it actually,' he confessed after a tiny pause.

She stared at him, her heart squeezing painfully, her throat suddenly dry. 'You…you don't believe me?'

He gave her an ironic smile. 'If it truly wasn't mine you would never have come within two stares of me. You hate me too much, remember?'

She shifted her gaze a fraction. 'If you want to have one done I won't stop you.'

'It's really not necessary, Carli.'

She didn't want to feel grateful for his show of trust, knowing it would make her even more vulnerable, but it moved her deeply that he believed her. So many men wouldn't.

'Thank you,' she mumbled.

'Gracious as usual,' he observed with a wry twist to his mouth.

She met his satirical look with a flash of resentment in her caramel-brown eyes. 'If I sound a little ungrateful you have only yourself to blame. You're the one who accused me of doing it deliberately.'

'I've already apologised for that,' he said. 'You can't keep dragging it out to flay me with.'

'How very convenient for you,' she sniped. 'You insult me and make some paltry attempt to apologise, not even going so far as to use those two little words: I'm sorry.'

'All right,' his voice rose in anger, 'I'm sorry. There— will that do?'

'You don't mean it.' She folded her arms crossly.

'Oh, for pity's sake, Carli, what the hell do you want me to do?' He was almost shouting now. 'Wasn't I allowed to be upset by your news? You came to my office and delivered your blunt statement with absolutely no lead up to it. Is it any wonder I spoke a little irrationally at the time?'

She knew he was right; she hadn't given him any warn-

ing and it *had* been a dreadful shock. She was still reeling
from it herself; God knew how he was feeling.

'I'm sorry…' She bit her lip, fighting back the sting of
tears.

He stepped towards her again, running his hand down
the length of her bare arm in a caressing stroke that brought
her glistening gaze back up to his.

'I'm sorry for shouting,' he said. 'I know it doesn't help
things between us but sometimes I just wish you'd listen
to my side.'

She stepped away before she was tempted to throw herself into his arms, and, picking up her handbag, turned for
the stairs.

'I want you to come with me tomorrow evening, Carli,'
he said. 'I want my parents to know we are living together.'

'So tell them.' She pivoted on the first step to look back
at him. 'I don't need to be there for you to do so.'

'Are you afraid of my family?' he asked, watching her
steadily.

'No, of course not. I just don't see the point in laying
myself open for criticism.'

'They won't criticise you. I can absolutely guarantee
that.'

'No?' She gave a harsh laugh. 'Not while you're around
maybe. I was well aware of the imperious looks as soon as
you introduced me as your future wife. No doubt their painfully polite restraints were lifted as soon as we parted. Bully
for you to have such a faithful crowd of supporters, I'm
sure it helped you get over me.'

Xavier's forehead creased in a frown at her words. It
hadn't been the first time he'd heard them, of course. In
the past she insisted his family had shut her out and made
fun of her behind her back, but he hadn't wanted to believe
it back then. It still shamed him to think it had taken a

further three years after their divorce for him to see his parents for what they were.

He looked across at the pinched features of his ex-wife and inwardly sighed. Her eyes were hollow with tiredness and her small frame looked even more fragile than the day she'd come to his office to tell him about the pregnancy. As much as he'd have liked to tell her he had come around to see her point of view at last, he didn't think it would change anything between them. It was clear she had nothing but disdain for him. He could see it in her eyes. Her gaze kept skittering away from his as if she couldn't bear to look at him.

He could hardly blame her.

'Your things arrived earlier and I had my housekeeper unpack everything into one of the spare rooms,' he informed her in a voice that showed nothing of his inner disquiet.

'Thank you,' she said and began to climb the stairs. 'But I could have done it myself.'

'Carli?'

She stopped and looked at him over her shoulder, her eyes not quite making the distance to his. 'Yes?'

'I know how hard this is for you, moving in with me and so on.'

'You don't say.'

He ignored her attempt at sarcasm and continued, 'Don't worry about my family. I won't let them come between us.'

Carli resumed her passage up the stairs without responding.

While his family had their issues with her, they weren't the only obstacle in the way of her relationship with Xavier.

He didn't love her.

That was the biggest obstacle of all.

# CHAPTER FOUR

ELEANOR and Bryce Knightly were excruciatingly polite to Carli when Xavier led her inside the Knightly family mansion at Vaucluse the following evening.

'Carla, my dear.' Eleanor air-kissed her cheek and pushed her husband forward. 'Isn't she looking marvellous, Bryce?'

'Indeed she is.' Bryce kissed her briefly and stood back. 'Your weight gain suits you.'

'Carli is pregnant,' Xavier announced without preamble.

That both his parents were shocked was clearly obvious, although to her credit Eleanor recovered herself quickly.

'But…but that's…wonderful news! I didn't know you'd married again. What is your new husband's name?'

'I don't have a husband,' Carli announced bluntly.

Eleanor Knightly put a fluttering hand up to her throat. 'Oh…I see.'

'The baby is mine,' Xavier said.

His mother looked at him in shock. 'Are you sure?'

Carli saw his jaw tighten as he answered, 'Absolutely.'

'Have you had a paternity test done,' Eleanor asked, 'just to remove all doubt?'

Carli resisted sending Xavier an I-told-you-so look even though she dearly longed to. She kept her eyes trained on his parents standing awkwardly before them, very conscious of Xavier's rigid form beside her.

'I am the baby's father, there is no doubt of that,' he stated implacably.

'When are you getting married again?' his father asked.

'We're not planning on remarrying,' Xavier said.

His mother's elegantly made-up face visibly blanched. 'Not getting remarried? But of course you must get remarried! What will everyone think?'

'I don't give a damn what people think,' he said. 'This is between Carli and me, no one else.'

'But surely with a child on the way…' Eleanor's voice faded at the intractable look in her son's eye.

'What would you like to drink?' Bryce did his best to lighten the tense atmosphere but Carli was already wishing the evening was over.

She couldn't believe the hypocrisy of Xavier's parents. She'd felt the sting of their disapproval from the very first time he'd introduced her, although they'd carefully hidden it behind a barrier of cool politeness whenever their son was around. It had caused many an argument between Xavier and her in the past. He had accused her of being paranoid while she had argued he was insensitive and blind-sided to the dynamics of his family.

His three younger sisters had been no better. She could still recall the snickering on one occasion when she'd turned up straight from university to what she had assumed was to be a family dinner. No one had told her it was a formal affair with several important guests from the Knightly legal firm who, along with Xavier's sisters, took in her torn jeans and tight-fitting T-shirt with noses wrinkling in collective distaste. Her pride had insisted she stay on regardless, but by the time Xavier had arrived her nerves were shredded to the point where she could barely speak. He'd sent her one or two questioning glances during the evening but it wasn't until they finally returned to his house that she let fly with all her pent-up feelings.

It had been a nasty scene…

* * *

Xavier had slammed the door behind him as they entered the house, the sound of it echoing right throughout the house.

'What the hell is the matter with you?' he bellowed as she stalked towards the stairs. 'Do you realise how embarrassing that was for me this evening? For God's sake, Carli, I have to work with those people, you know.'

'*You* were embarrassed?' She spun around in outrage. 'How do you think I felt with your sneering, snobby sisters making me feel like a bit of trailer trash all evening?'

'Well, if you choose to turn up at my parents' house dressed like that, what else do you expect?' he countered, running his eyes over her too-tight T-shirt.

She stared at him in fury. 'No one told me it was a formal affair.' She bit out each word individually.

'My mother told me she'd called you.'

'Your mother lied,' she said, her hands going to her hips in an aggressive pose. 'Now, who are you going to believe, your mother or your wife?'

He gave her a contemptuous look and ground out, 'You act more like a spoilt brat than a wife so that decision is going to be way too easy.' He tossed his coat to one side and continued before she could speak, 'I know what you were up to tonight, Carli. You wanted to embarrass my father and me and our colleagues so you could drive home another one of your feminist points, but in doing so you just shot yourself in the foot.'

'I did not—'

'No one is going to take you seriously until you grow up a bit,' he interrupted her denial. 'I thought I married a young, intelligent woman and instead I keep coming home to a petulant child who can't even control her own temper.'

Carli hadn't really realised just how angry she was until

the first vase hit the wall next to Xavier's head, shattering into a thousand pieces.

The silence was so thick she could almost reach out and touch it. It seemed to move across the space that divided them, great invisible swirls of it coming up to her to steal her breath out of her lungs as she saw the flashing ire in Xavier's midnight-blue gaze as it locked on to hers.

She knew she'd gone way too far but somehow, as if it had a mind of its own, her hand reached for the other vase.

'I wouldn't if I were you,' he cautioned, his tone like cold, hard steel. 'You might not like the consequences.'

She told him exactly what she thought of his stupid consequences and threw it anyway, watching with a perverse sort of satisfaction as he flinched out of the way of the priceless missile as it sailed past his right ear.

He stepped over the smashed porcelain on the floor without a word, moving towards her with steady but controlled purpose…

'Champagne, Carla?' Bryce's forced cheerfulness brought her back to the present with a jarring jolt.

She stared at him blankly for what seemed endless seconds before Xavier answered for her. 'No alcohol for Carli.'

'A little bit won't hurt, surely,' Eleanor said.

Carli saw the look Xavier cast his mother's way and inwardly grimaced. Things were not very harmonious in the Knightly family and it begged the question why.

Eleanor did her best to maintain her poise but it was impossible not to see the strain etched around her carefully lipstick-painted mouth.

'Did Xavier tell you Phoebe, Imogen and Harriet are all studying for degrees?' Bruce said in an attempt to fill the awkward silence.

Carli's gaze flicked briefly to Xavier's before returning to his father's. 'No…he didn't happen to mention it.' She was beginning to think there was a whole lot he hadn't told her about his family dynamics, both past and present.

'I've never understood why they feel the need to complicate their lives with university lectures and assignments,' Eleanor said. 'God knows it's already put Harriet's marriage under intolerable strain. Neil has threatened to leave numerous times but she just won't listen.'

'Why wouldn't he want his wife to reach her full potential?' Carli put in before she could stop herself.

Eleanor's mouth opened and closed as if she wasn't quite sure how to answer.

'So,' Bryce took a restorative sip of his brandy and swiftly changed the subject, 'what have you been doing with yourself, Carla? Working for some big law firm by now, I expect.'

Carli was almost certain Bryce knew exactly where she worked and had only asked the question to yet again highlight the differences between her and Xavier.

'As you know, Bryce, it is extremely rare for young women to be offered partnerships,' she said, 'particularly in the larger city firms.'

Bryce looked as if he would like to argue the point further but Xavier put his arm around Carli's shoulders and drew her close.

'Come on, Dad. Let's not stir up a hornets' nest. Carli and I are here to announce our pregnancy and the fact that we've decided to live together. I don't want her upset.'

Carli knew his concern was primarily for the baby she carried but she still felt a rush of warmth at his protective words. Had he too been remembering that dreadful argument that had been the death knell for their marriage?

All through the elaborate dinner the Knightly housekeeper had prepared with her usual fastidious detail Carli could sense the undercurrents of tension at the table. She made her way through the overly rich meal very conscious of the stilted conversation passing between Xavier and his parents. She chanced a glance at Eleanor, who appeared to be having even less success with consuming the meal than she was.

Bryce did his level best to keep things flowing but Carli noticed the way he constantly topped up his wine glass as if it gave him a reprieve from facing the steely glare of his only son across the table.

Once dessert was cleared away they moved through to the spacious lounge, where coffee and chocolates were laid out before them.

Carli longed to leave the stiff and formal atmosphere but forced herself to endure the lengthy silences broken only by the occasional clatter of a paper-thin bone-china cup against its saucer.

After what seemed an interminable time Xavier got to his feet and reached for Carli's hand, drawing her up to stand beside him as he addressed his parents. 'We should get going. I have an early start in the morning and Carli is just about dead on her feet.'

'Yes…of course.' Eleanor's overly bright smile didn't quite hide the relief washing over her face in waves.

Bryce joined his wife at the door to wave them off but Carli couldn't help noticing the door had closed even before Xavier had backed out of the driveway.

Carli turned back to the front and worried her bottom lip for a moment.

'Did you find tonight an ordeal?' Xavier asked after a pause.

'It was…interesting.'

She felt his glance swing her way.

'In what way?'

She looked back at him. 'Your parents don't seem all that comfortable around you any more. Have you had some sort of falling-out?'

His eyes went back to the road ahead but he didn't respond until he'd shifted through the gears to move through the intersection.

'You could say that.'

'What was it about?' she asked.

'This and that.'

'Was this or that anything to do with me?'

Carli felt as if a full minute passed before he answered, as if he was mentally rehearsing his response before he delivered it.

'It took me a while to realise the shallowness of my parents' lives. They measure people according to wealth and social status, not character or moral fibre. It struck me one day that unless I did something about it I could very well end up exactly like them.' He flicked a wry glance towards her. 'You, of course, had already seen the likeness.'

Carli sat in a stunned silence.

'My mother made some derogatory comment about you a couple of years back. I guess it wasn't anything she hadn't said before, but somehow this time I saw how it must have been for you. You were so young and inexperienced, no match for any of the Knightlys.'

'Including you?' she asked, her voice a thin thread of sound.

He waited until he'd parked in his garage and killed the engine before turning to look at her. 'Including me.'

Carli felt the magnetic pull of his intense gaze as it rested on her face and watched in silence as he lifted the back of his hand to graze his knuckles along the soft curve of her cheek.

'And here you are, back in the firing line,' he said, 'all because of a simple twist of fate.'

She moistened her mouth with her tongue, her breath hitching in her throat as his eyes followed its movement. His eyes darkened measurably as his head came down, his warm breath a soft caress as he pressed his mouth to hers.

She sighed as his lips moved over hers, one of his hands sliding under the heavy curtain of her hair to bring her head closer still. She felt the probe of his tongue and opened her mouth on another sigh as he sought her moistness in slow-moving strokes that set her instantly on fire. She felt the sudden leap of her pulse, the shiver of reaction along her spine as he deepened the kiss even further, the searching stroke of his tongue drawing a sigh of pure pleasure from deep within her. She kissed him back without restraint, her teeth scraping along the surface of his in her desperate need to have more of him, her tongue mating with his, the primal urge so strong she had no control over it.

One of his hands found her breast, skilfully lifting her top out of the way, his fingers stroking over the tight nipple in little circles that sent arrows of sensation through her belly. Her breasts had always been sensitive to his touch but with the surge of pregnancy hormones in her system the pleasure was almost unbearable.

Xavier pulled back and looked down at her uptilted face and passion-glazed eyes. 'Why don't we take this indoors?'

Carli felt rationality seep back into her veins where the heady throb of passion had just been. What had she been thinking—that things between them would magically return to harmony as if the last five years hadn't existed?

Yes, he'd finally seen his parents in a realistic light but that didn't change the fact that he didn't love her any more.

She knew he wouldn't have re-entered her life if she hadn't told him about the pregnancy. The Xavier she'd known in the past would have let no one stand in his way if he'd wanted something. It wouldn't have mattered that he'd made some vague promise to leave her alone. If he'd truly cared he would have been on her doorstep the very next day. Instead, four long months had passed and not a single word.

'No,' she said.

'No as in let's finish it here, or no as in no?' he asked.

She met his eyes determinedly. 'No as in no.'

'I see.'

She opened her door but within seconds he was around her side, his expression grim and his tone sliding into bitterness. 'I suppose this is your way to get back at me. Even though you want me you're prepared to punish yourself in the process of extracting revenge.'

'I told you before I'm not interested in a physical relationship with you,' she said, pushing away from the car.

'You're carrying my child, for God's sake!' He strode angrily beside her as she made her way to the house. 'What are you doing, saving yourself for someone special?'

Carli swung around to glare at him. 'Yes, as a matter of fact, I am waiting for someone special.'

'Oh, really? Anyone I might know?' His tone was deliberately mocking. 'Maybe I should have a couple of beers with him to let him know what he's in for.' He opened the front door and held it open for her, adding, 'Does he know about your propensity for violence when you get pushed into a corner?'

Carli reined in her temper with an effort. 'I don't wish to continue this conversation.'

'No, of course you don't. You don't like being in the

guilty seat, do you? That's been set aside for me all these years.'

'If the seat fits, sit in it,' she bit out.

She brushed past him to make her way upstairs but he snagged one of her arms on the way past and turned her to face him. 'I did my best, Carli. I worked my butt off for us both but it wasn't enough for you. You wanted what I couldn't give.'

She pulled herself out of his hold. 'Yes, because, while you gave me everything money could buy, there was one thing you just wouldn't give—yourself.'

'I suppose you're going to let me know in intimate detail all the times I neglected to tell you of my feelings and when I didn't demonstrate enough affection or say the right words. What you wanted was a cardboard cut-out of the perfect husband. Some sort of puppet to pander to your ever-changing needs. But I'm not a puppet, Carli; I'm a man with real feelings and issues just like everybody else. So I got it wrong a few times, who doesn't? You didn't get it right all that often yourself. There were so many times when I wanted to tell you of what I was facing at work but I didn't because I knew you were so focused on what *you* needed, you didn't give a damn for what was going on in my life.'

'That's not true! I was always there for you!'

He gave her a look of disdain as he loosened his tie. 'Were you?'

She lowered her eyes, suddenly uncomfortable with the weight of his steely gaze.

'You were always going on about the injustice of it all. How marriage was an institution designed to keep women under the thumb. Did you ever stop to think that maybe I had to face certain injustices as well?' He shrugged himself out of his jacket and flung it to one side. 'I had to provide for you while you were studying, but did I ever complain? I worked eighty-hour weeks to build our future. Little did I know you were putting in double that time behind my back to destroy it.'

'Our marriage only had room for one career and that was yours,' she threw back bitterly. 'I just wish you'd told me it was going to be that way before I married you.'

'Oh, for Christ's sake, Carli. What the hell did you want me to do—list down all the possible outcomes of our relationship just so you could prepare yourself?'

'I did my best…' She compressed her lips together, valiantly fighting the urge to cry.

'Well, maybe your best just wasn't good enough.' He tossed his keys to the hall table, their metallic clatter as they landed jarring her overstretched nerves.

He strode past her up the stairs. 'Make yourself at home; I'm sure you know where everything is by now. Goodnight.'

Carli watched in silence as he disappeared from sight, the heaviness of his accusation keeping her pinned to the spot in sudden, crushing guilt.


When Carli came downstairs the next morning Xavier was standing at the kitchen counter sipping a cup of coffee while he read the morning paper. He looked up when she came in and, putting his cup down, straightened to his full height.

'Carli, about last night…' He paused as if searching for the right words to say. 'It was wrong of me to pressure you.' He ran a hand through his hair, disturbing its early-morning neatness. 'Old habits die hard, to use an ironic choice of words.'

'It's OK.' She could feel the warm colour creeping into her cheeks but held his gaze regardless.

'No, it's not OK. You have the right to say no. At all times and under any circumstances, we both know the law on that one.' His eyes left her momentarily to glance at his watch. 'I have to be in court in the hour. I'll call you during the day.'

'You don't have to bother.'

He came around the counter to tip up her chin so she had to look at him. 'Hey, it's no bother. Got that?'

She gave the small nod his hold allowed. 'Got that.'

'Good girl.' He tapped her on the end of her nose and stepped away. 'Look after that baby of mine, OK?'

She did her best to smile although her face ached with the effort. 'I will.'

The drive to her place of work was agonisingly slow, the early heat of the January morning escalating to such a degree that her clothes were completely damp by the time she arrived.

She felt flustered and uncomfortable and for the first time began to notice how run-down and shabby the offices were. To make matters worse, each and every client who trailed through the door seemed to be intent on having her run ragged in pursuit of their particular idea of justice.

At mid-morning she thought longingly of a plush suite of offices with a harbour view, and by mid-afternoon was dreaming of air-conditioning that functioned as it should and a secretary who could actually spell.

By the time six o'clock came she was almost asleep at her desk.

She pushed the tedious paperwork aside and got to her feet and stretched, wincing as a deep pain in her abdomen caught her off guard.

She gripped the edge of the desk and took several deep breaths, doing her best to keep control of her rising panic.

The telephone rang beside her and in between breaths she reached to pick it up. 'Carla Gresham.'

'Carli, it's me.' Xavier's deep voice sounded in her ear.

'Hello…'

'You sound breathless.'

'It's…hot.'

'Thirty-seven in the shade,' he informed her. 'What's it like out in the west?'

'There's no shade.'

'As bad as that?' Amusement leaked into his tone. 'What time will you be home?'

Home.

How normal he made it sound!

'If all goes well, in about an hour.' She sucked in another breath as the pain hit her again.

'Are you all right?' he asked.

'I'm…fine.'

'You sound…weird.'

'Thank you.'

'I didn't mean it like that,' he said. 'Hard day at the office?'

'No more than usual.'

'Why don't you wait there and I'll pick you up?'

She clung to her independence even though she was touched by his concern. But then she remembered how much he wanted the baby and knew the concern had very little to do with her personally; it was the baby he was thinking of, not her.

'I'm leaving right this minute anyway so don't bother.'

'It's no bother.'

'I need the drive home to relax.'

'If you find driving in Sydney traffic relaxing then there is something seriously wrong with you,' he said drily.

'There's nothing wrong with me!' she insisted.

'Drive safely, then,' he said. 'That's my baby you've got on board there.'

'How could I ever forget?' she asked and plonked the phone back down before he could respond.

Xavier stared at the receiver in his hand and wondered if he should ring her back and insist on having his way, but before he could press redial his secretary poked her head around the door and held out a file to him.

'Here's the Dangar file you asked for,' she said. 'But let me tell you he's not going to be too happy about you handing him over to Michael. He wants you and only you.'

Xavier sighed as he took the file. 'Leave it with me. I'll call him tomorrow and see if I can change his mind.'

Elaine folded her arms across her ample chest and surveyed his darkly handsome features. 'So...are you going to tell me why you're not going to act for him?'

'It's none of your business.'

'Can I take a guess?' Elaine's light blue eyes twinkled knowingly.

'If you must.'

'Well...since I've never known you to hand over a case before, I'm assuming it's because of someone you don't want to lock heads with.'

'Go on.'

'Would that someone be your ex-wife?'

He leant back in his chair and gave his pen a click. 'Why don't you go home to that husband of yours and get out his pipe and slippers like all good wives should be doing at this hour?'

Elaine gave him a mischievous grin. 'Is that what you expect Carli to do now that she's come home to you?'

He gave her a scowl as he pushed back his chair to get up. 'Carli would love to give me a pipe and slippers but I'm not sure she'd put them exactly where I wanted them.'

'She's a sweet little thing,' Elaine said with one finger on her chin in a musing pose. 'Makes me kind of wonder how you two ever got together in the first place.'

'Meaning?' One dark brow came up in an arc.

Elaine shifted her weight to one generous hip. 'You still love her, don't you?'

Xavier's frown deepened. 'I pay you to keep my public life organised, not to pry into my private life.'

'I can't organise your public life if your private life is a mess,' Elaine pointed out with legal expertise.

'My private life is not a mess.'

'Isn't it?' she asked and before he could respond she closed the office door, locking him in with his denial hovering on his lips.

Carli decided at the last minute to call in at her doctor's surgery, for even though the pain she'd experienced had gone, she couldn't help feeling worried in case something was going wrong with her pregnancy.

Dr Green was reassuring but realistic. 'Carli, a pregnancy isn't always as straightforward as one would hope. You're in reasonably good health but with the amount of hours you're currently working you're asking a lot of yourself. Your blood pressure is slightly elevated, which isn't good for you or the baby. Have you considered taking some time off work? A week or two would make all the difference at this stage.'

'I don't know…'

'What about your personal life?' the doctor asked. 'I realise your relationship with the baby's father is somewhat complicated. Have you come to some sort of arrangement with him?'

'Sort of,' she answered, wondering what the doctor would say if she was to tell her of Xavier's ultimatum to get her to live with him. An ultimatum she had snatched at with two greedy, desperate hands.

'Well, my advice is to have a couple of weeks' rest. Come and see me after that and if your health hasn't improved you may have to consider working part-time until the baby comes.'

Carli left the doctor's surgery and made her way to Xavier's house, wondering how her life had become so terribly complicated. Four months ago she had been single and career-driven, her work her entire focus, morning noon and night. Meeting Xavier again had changed everything, turning her ordered life upside down in the blink of an eye. Her career aspirations had taken a nosedive to make room for the baby she carried, with all her ideals fading away as if they'd never been.

She couldn't imagine what Xavier would say if he was to find out how far she had moved from the very ideals that had caused their marriage to break up in the first place.

It just didn't bear thinking about.

# CHAPTER FIVE

XAVIER paced the lounge room for half an hour, his neck feeling tight from all the times he'd glanced down at his watch.

Where was she?

He'd called her mobile but it kept switching through to her answering service and his concern ratcheted up another notch. What if she'd had an accident? She might be lying somewhere bleeding...

The front door opened and before he could stop himself he flung down his glass and strode out into the hall.

'What the hell has taken you so long?'

Carli flinched at the volume and tone of his voice, her hand going automatically to her abdomen.

His eyes followed her nervous movement and he raked a hand through his hair in a distracted manner.

'I was worried,' he added gruffly. 'I didn't mean to shout.'

'I stopped off at the doctor's.'

He stiffened. 'What for? Is something wrong?'

'I had a pain...'

'Where?'

'Here.' Her hand touched her belly.

'The baby?' He frowned.

'The baby is fine,' she reassured him. 'I just need to take things a little easier, that's all.'

'Why don't you go and lie down and I'll bring you up some dinner?' he suggested. 'My housekeeper has left something for us in the oven; it won't take long to put it on a tray.'

'Please don't bother. I just want to go to bed.'

'Carli, either you have something to eat or I'll insist on you cutting back on your workload. You're exhausted and putting our child at risk by not taking better care of yourself.'

'Look, I've already had this lecture from the doctor half an hour ago,' she said. 'I don't need another one from you.'

'What did the doctor say?'

She sighed as she kicked off her shoes, deciding at the last minute not to tell him of the two weeks off work the doctor had advised. 'My blood pressure is a bit high; that's why my ankles are a bit swollen.'

His eyes went to her feet and he frowned. 'Isn't that dangerous for the baby?'

'It is in the long term.'

'What will you do?' he asked, picking up her shoes for her.

'I don't know.' She sighed again. 'I have a lot of work right now; I can't imagine trying to cram it all into a part-time position.'

'Can I help you with anything?'

She met his concerned gaze and couldn't help a wry smile. 'Somehow I can't quite see you sitting in my run-down office listening to all the hard-luck stories that wander through the door. You'd better stick to your Armani clients, Xavier; it's pretty wild out there in the west.'

'The law is the law in the city or the suburbs,' he pointed out.

She gave him a cynical look. 'The only difference being, of course, that in the city people can pay for justice, and those in the outer suburbs can't. You're a white-collar lawyer, Xavier, just like your father and grandfather before you. But there are thousands of worthwhile people out in blue-collar land who deserve justice just as much as if not more than those with higher incomes.'

'So you've sacrificed your career aspirations to help them?'

'Not intentionally,' she said. 'But somehow the rest of the legal profession looks down on what legal-aid lawyers do as if we're not good enough to work in more salaried positions.'

'I'm aware of that bias but I don't necessarily share it.'

'Don't you?' she asked. 'But you still think I'm underselling myself all the same.'

'I think you're overworking yourself,' he clarified. 'There's a difference. Now, go upstairs and I'll be up soon with your dinner.'

She was sitting up in bed, freshly showered and feeling much more human, when he shouldered open the door half an hour later carrying a tray. He set it down across her knees and the aroma of a Provençal-style lamb casserole began to tease her nostrils.

He sat on the edge of the bed and handed her the cutlery. 'Now eat.'

She gave him a resentful scowl from beneath her lowered lashes. 'Do you have to sit there and watch me?'

'I like watching you.'

'I can't imagine why.' She poked at a juicy cube of lamb and popped it into her mouth.

'It's very entertaining watching you try and defy me when deep down what you really want to do is give in.'

'And I suppose you think all women want a masterful male in their life so they don't have to think for themselves any more?'

'No, I don't think that at all, but I do know you often fight me when your real opponent is yourself. Why beat yourself up about it? There's no shame in needing someone.'

'I do not need you.'

'So you like to tell me but we both know it's not true. Why else would you have come to me that day to tell me about the baby?'

'You had a right to know...' She stabbed at another cube of meat with vicious intent.

'You came to me to help you,' he said. 'You could have easily got rid of the pregnancy without me knowing a thing but you didn't. Instead you came to me.'

'I've always had a problem with late abortions.'

He gave her a long, probing look. 'If you'd found out any earlier, would you have terminated it?'

She held his look without wavering. 'No.'

'You didn't need to tell me. You could have pretended it was someone else's and got on with your life. Why did you contact me?'

She chased a piece of carrot around her plate without answering.

'Do you want me to tell you what I think?' he asked.

She gave up on the carrot and pursued a short stem of celery instead. 'No, but I'm sure you're going to tell me anyway.'

'I think deep down you wanted me to solve the dilemma you were in. As much as you hate to admit it, you came to me to help you deal with something bigger than you could handle. You slipped into the helpless-female role with ease.'

'I am not helpless and I don't need you to solve any-thing.' She put down her fork and pushed the tray away.

One of his hands came over hers and brought the tray back. He took the fork and speared a succulent piece of lamb and held it close to her mouth as if feeding a small child. 'Open,' he commanded.

She glowered at him but opened her mouth all the same.

'Good girl.' He scooped up some more. 'And again.'

Before she knew it the plate was empty but instead of feeling nauseous she felt comfortably satisfied.

'That wasn't so hard, now, was it?' He smiled as he removed the tray from her lap.

She hated admitting he was right but could hardly dispute an empty plate. She gave him a sheepish look and fiddled with the edge of the sheet.

'I haven't felt like eating for ages,' she said. 'I think it's the heat.'

'You used to love the hot weather.' He handed her the glass of juice off the tray.

She took a sip before answering. 'I know…but since I've been pregnant I feel different about lots of things.'

'Any cravings?'

Only for you, she wanted to say.

'No…'

'Let me know if you fancy anything special and I'll make sure you have it.'

'You're being very…nice about all this.' She gave the sheet another pluck.

'I have a vested interest.' He gave her a teasing smile.

'A lot of men find the prospect of fatherhood very threatening,' she said.

'I have heard some talk of that but I can't say I identify with it. I find the prospect of bringing a child into the world an amazing privilege, one that I wasn't sure I was going to have.'

'But surely you would have remarried eventually?'

He shrugged as he took her now empty glass. 'I wasn't planning on making the same mistake twice.'

'You could still have had a child without having to marry,' she pointed out.

'I know, but none of the women I was involved with was too taken with the idea and not just because of their career.'

'It's a big decision to have a baby, career or not.'

'And because of me you didn't get the chance to make it for yourself,' he said.

She frowned at the self-reproach in his tone.

'You didn't do it alone,' she said softly.

His eyes came back to hers.

'No, I didn't, but it still doesn't change the fact that I should have been more responsible.'

'It was a mistake…' She ran her tongue over her lips in a nervous gesture. 'We were in an emotionally charged state because of the lift. On another day it never would have happened.'

'You think so?' His dark gaze pulled hers back.

She swallowed. 'Of…of course…'

'You don't sound all that convinced.'

She tore her eyes away and stared at the rumpled sheet once more. 'You can't imagine how shocked I was afterwards. Shocked and ashamed.'

'I wasn't too happy myself,' he admitted, 'but not for those reasons.'

She looked at him once more. 'What do you mean?'

His eyes darkened as they flicked down to her mouth. 'I was angry with myself for days for not coming after you and telling you how much I enjoyed being with you in the lift.'

'*You enjoyed that?*' She gaped at him incredulously.

'I had you to myself for the first time in five years. I was almost disappointed when the rescue team arrived.'

'You can't mean that!'

'It's true,' he said. 'Think about it, Carli. When had we ever talked like that before?'

A tiny frown settled between her brows at his statement, and a funny sensation settled in her chest at the realisation of the element of truth behind his words.

They *had* talked during their time in the jammed lift; they'd argued too, but…

'I don't recall a single time when we discussed our life goals or what we would do if that day was our very last,' he said. 'We were always too busy fighting over stupid, inconsequential details such as who had the biggest pay packet.'

'Those were still important issues,' she said.

'Maybe, but not in the big scheme of things. What did it matter who was earning what? The thing we should have been focusing on was being together, building a secure future for our children.'

'If you remember, I didn't want to have children.'

He went very still and the sudden silence compressed the air in the room until Carli found it hard to draw in a breath.

'One hopes you've changed your mind or we have a much bigger problem than I first realised,' he said with a touch of dryness.

'When I found out I was pregnant I was furious,' she confessed. 'I couldn't believe something like that could happen, but over time I started to think about the baby…'

'And now?' he asked.

'To be quite truthful, if the choice had been left up to me I might never have had the courage to commit myself to a pregnancy. But now I can't help feeling as if this was somehow meant to be. Does that make sense to you?'

He grazed the smooth skin of her cheek with the back of his hand. 'It makes perfect sense to me.'

She touched her cheek with her own fingers. 'Why did you do that?'

'I like the feel of your skin,' he said, touching her again. 'It makes me think of silk and roses.'

She turned her head and pressed her mouth to the palm of his hand in a soft kiss.

'Why did you do that?' he asked.

She held his intent look for a pulsing moment. 'Because I wanted to.'

'Why?'

'I like your hands.'

He gave her a soft smile as he cupped her face. 'I think I should go before I'm tempted to let my hands do things they have no business doing. I gave you my word after all.'

She drew in a breath that tugged at her chest all the way down.

'Goodnight, Carli.' He pressed a soft kiss to the side of her mouth and stood up.

She stared at him as he reached for the tray he'd put aside earlier, her emotions ricocheting off the tender surface of her heart.

'Goodnight,' she choked as he closed the door behind him.

'I love you,' she whispered but he'd already moved well past the range of hearing.

She sank back to the pillows and thumped her fist down beside her.

'Damn!'

Carli phoned her office the next morning to tell them she wouldn't be in for the next two weeks and had only just put the receiver down when Xavier sauntered into her room with breakfast on a tray.

'Haven't you heard of knocking?' She gave him a chilly

look as she dragged the sheet up a bit higher to cover herself.

'Good morning to you too,' he drawled as he laid the tray across her lap. 'What's made you so grumpy this fine morning?'

'Nothing. I just think you should knock before you come wandering in.'

'I was going to send Mrs Fingleton up with your breakfast but somehow thought you might prefer me since I'm not exactly a complete stranger, but it seems I was mistaken.' He turned to leave the room and was almost at the door before she found her voice.

'Xavier?'

He turned around and gave her a bored look. 'Look, Carli, I'm going to be late for court if I don't leave in the next two minutes. I'll see you this evening.'

The door closed behind him with a thump that sent a shockwave through the tea in her cup. Carli stared down at the disturbed surface of hot liquid until it finally settled, wondering if she would ever get used to living without his love…

She made her way downstairs and, after briefly introducing herself to the housekeeper, left the house to pay an impromptu visit to Eliza Dangar in Hunters Hill.

The morning traffic had eased and she pulled up in front of the gracious home of her friend, remonstrating with herself for leaving it so long before visiting her.

As she walked up the path to the front door she couldn't help noticing the normally immaculate garden was looking neglected, the weeds outnumbering the flowers and shrubs, the lawn more brown than green and the edges untrimmed like a fringe grown too long.

She pressed the doorbell and when no one answered she

walked around to the back of the house, checking the garage to see if Eliza's car was there.

The family sedan was parked in its usual place, the child seats side by side in the back. She frowned and turned to make her way to the back door when she heard the faint sound of a baby crying from inside the house.

'Eliza?' She tapped on the door. 'Are you in there?'

It seemed a long time before the door was opened and when it was Carli nearly fell over backwards in shock at Eliza's appearance. Her friend's normally curvaceous figure was gaunt to the point of emaciation, her usually shiny brown hair lank and scraped back unflatteringly from her face.

'Eliza...are you all right?'

'Of course I'm all right,' Eliza said with a hint of defensiveness to her tone. 'Why didn't you call first to tell me you were coming? I'm not really prepared for visitors.'

'Hey, honey,' Carli gave her a mock-reproachful look, 'it's me—Carli. You don't have to hide the basket of ironing from me.'

Eliza opened the door to let her come in and Carli was immediately appalled by the staleness of the air inside the house, the smell of unwashed nappies predominating.

'Where are the kids?' Carli asked.

'Amelia's at preschool this morning,' Eliza answered. 'Brody's supposed to be sleeping but won't settle.'

Just then the sound of the infant crying began again in earnest and Carli gave her friend a 'may I?' glance before going to him, doing her best to overlook the general disorder of the normally tidy to the point of perfection house.

'Hey there, little man, what's all this fuss about?' Carli cooed as she picked him up, and as she held him against her a wave of tenderness swept through her as he rested his tear-washed little face against her neck. She stroked his back and rocked from side to side, singing a little song she dredged from the far reaches of her brain, a song her mother had once sung to her in the days before depression had stripped all music from her personality.

The decline of her friend's appearance was a painful reminder of the enveloping sadness which had eventually consumed her mother. She could even recall the same disorder of her childhood home. She couldn't remember a day during her school years when she hadn't come home to a sink full of dirty dishes, unwashed clothes and her mother's strained, unhappy features staring vacantly into space.

Once Brody was asleep she laid him gently in his cot and returned to the kitchen, where Eliza was sitting smoking a cigarette.

Carli frowned and immediately opened the nearest window. 'Since when did you start smoking?' she asked, wrinkling her nose in distaste.

Eliza gave her an up-and-down look and took in another deep drag before retorting with uncharacteristic bitchiness, 'Since when did you start putting on weight?'

Carli took the bull by the horns and announced bluntly, 'Since I got pregnant.'

Eliza's cigarette's smoke curled like a question mark in the air in front of her astonished face. '*You're pregnant?*' she gasped. '*You?*'

Carli nodded.

'Well, I'll be damned…' Eliza stubbed out her cigarette. 'Who's the father?'

'You wouldn't believe me if I told you.'

'Try me.'

Carli took a shallow breath on account of the lingering smoke and said, 'Xavier.'

Eliza's eyes positively bulged with shock. 'You're having me on…aren't you?'

Carli shook her head.

'*Christ.*'

'That's exactly what Xavier said when I told him,' Carli said wryly.

'How the hell did it happen?'

'The usual way.'

'You know what I mean,' Eliza said. 'How the blazes did you two end up in bed together after, what is it now…five years since the divorce?'

Carli found it hard to hold her friend's questioning look. 'It just happened…it shouldn't have…but it did.'

'I thought you hated his guts.' Eliza reached for another cigarette. 'You've been head girl of the all-men-are-bastards school of thought ever since the divorce.'

'I did hate him…or at least I thought I did.'

'You still love him, don't you?'

Carli sat on the chair nearest the window before she answered. 'Love isn't an emotion you can switch on and off whenever you feel like it.'

'Tell me about it.' Eliza took another drag.

'You feel the same way about Aidan?' Carli guessed.

Eliza inspected the burning tip of her cigarette, the line of her mouth sad. 'You don't need me to tell you I'm not the woman he married. It's no wonder he's found someone else.'

Carli felt a lump constrict her throat. 'He's having an affair?'

Eliza tossed the cigarette into the sink, the tiny hiss of it extinguishing suddenly loud in the quiet room.

'Who could blame him?' she asked. 'I'm not exactly wife of the year, am I?

'You're run-down,' Carli said. 'You've not long had a baby; it's not fair to expect a new mother to have everything in perfect order all the time.'

Tears sprouted in Eliza's eyes and she brushed at them with a shaky hand. 'I can't go on like this, Carli, I just can't.'

Carli came over and enveloped her in a hug, stroking the back of her head in comfort, fighting back her own tears. 'You'll get through this...I know you will.'

Eliza wriggled out of Carli's embrace and stood some distance from her. 'How am I going to get through this? You're damn well sleeping with the enemy, for God's sake!'

Carli frowned at the venom in her friend's tone. 'What are you talking about?'

'You said you'd speak to Xavier about dropping the case. Little did I know you'd be doing so side by side in his bed.'

'I'm not sleeping with Xavier.'

Eliza's eyes flicked to the mound of Carli's belly. 'Are you telling me you had a one-night stand with your ex-husband?'

'It's complicated...but we have a sort of...arrangement.'

'What sort of arrangement?'

'I'm living with him but we're not...you know...'

Eliza let her breath out from between her teeth. 'And how long do you think that will last? What's wrong with you, Carli? Have you forgotten what happened five years ago? He broke your heart.'

'I can look after myself,' she said with far more conviction than she felt.

'Yeah, well, I used to say that too, and look what happened to me.'

'What has happened to you, Eliza?' Carli asked gently.

Eliza's thin shoulders slumped as she sat back down in her chair. 'I don't know...I used to be so organised, so happy and carefree, then bit by bit I started losing the plot…I'd scream at Amelia—I even hit her once—and Brody drives me nuts when he cries.' She put her head in her hands. 'I hate myself. I can't sleep, I can't eat…I feel so edgy all the time, I have panic attacks just going to the supermarket, and my heart feels like it's going to burst through my chest at times.'

'Have you seen a doctor?'

Eliza lifted her head to look at her. 'I'm not going to a psychiatrist.'

'I meant your GP. Have you considered there might be something wrong? You could have postnatal depression or even a hormonal imbalance.'

'A diagnosis isn't going to save my marriage, Carli, especially with Xavier Knightly acting for Aidan.'

'Xavier isn't acting for Aidan,' she said. 'He told me so.'

Eliza gave her a cynical look. 'And I suppose he also told you he's going to stick around once the baby's born? Don't be a fool, Carli. I had a phone call from Aidan this morning before you arrived. He told me Xavier is going to take the kids off me. It's as good as done. I don't stand a chance.'

Carli felt her throat close over in shock. Xavier had lied to her! He'd made her think he was going to hand over the case to someone else when all the time he had no intention of doing so. It had all been a ploy, a clever, devious, despicable ploy to get her to live with him once more.

Anger pumped through her veins so heavily she had trouble disguising her reaction from Eliza, who was quite clearly in no fit state to deal with her own emotions let alone someone else's.

'Look…' She took a calming breath and began picking up the dirty dishes off the table. 'Let's do a bit of a tidy-up around here while I think about this.'

'What's to think about?' Eliza scowled as she got to her

feet and stacked three glasses on top of each other. 'It's over.'

Carli wished she could think of something reassuring to say but nothing came to mind. Instead she gave her friend a quick hug on the way past to the sink and began washing up as if her life depended on it.

Several hours later Eliza's house was as near to spotless as it had ever been. Carli drove home in tired satisfaction, her greatest achievement of the day being to secure a promise from Eliza to attend an appointment scheduled with a local GP for the following day.

Later that evening she paced the lounge-room floor, waiting for Xavier to return, her temper rising with each passing minute.

Finally she heard his car pull into the garage and soon after the sound of his footsteps coming into the house.

She stalked across the room and, leaning on the door jamb in an imitation of his customary indolent pose, asked, 'Nice day at work, Xavier?'

His eyes ran over her briefly before returning to her face, his expression slightly guarded. 'I wouldn't have described it as such but it was no worse than any other. How about yours?'

'I had a very interesting day.' She gave him a pointed look. 'Very interesting indeed.'

He compressed his lips together for a moment. 'I get the distinct impression there's some sort of hidden agenda to this conversation. Why don't you save me the mental task of figuring it out and tell me for yourself?'

'It shouldn't be too hard to work out,' she said. 'After all, you're supposed to be the hot-shot lawyer who can spot a fake a mile off.'

'Look, Carli, I've had a long and trying day. Why not

cut with the games and tell me what's got you all hot under the collar?'

'You lied to me!'

He frowned as he shrugged himself out of his jacket. 'On which occasion was this?'

'You mean there was more than one?' She glared at him.

'Don't twist my words. I simply want to know what's upset you.'

'You said you were going to drop the Dangar case and pass it to someone else. You used that promise as a lure to get me here and now I'm here you've reneged on the deal.'

'You seem very sure about that.'

'Of course I'm sure! You lied as surely as you're standing there. Don't tell me you're going to deny it? Are you or are you not still acting for Aidan Dangar?'

His eyes moved away from the flashing anger in hers.

'It is customary to consult with the client before changing anything to do with the case.'

'You're evading the question.'

'I have no need to evade the question. I haven't as yet been in personal contact with Aidan. I had it on my list of things to do but I've been in court for most of the day and I left it with my secretary to make the necessary arrangements. Whether she has done so or not is something I can't answer right at this moment.'

Carli swung away in fury. 'I don't believe you.'

'That is entirely your affair, of course,' he answered smoothly.

'What was your plan?' She turned back to glare at him. 'To get me back into your house preparatory to getting me back in your bed?'

His eyes met the fiery heat of hers with consummate ease.

'That would really be a case of locking the stable door

after the horse had already bolted, don't you think?' His eyes dipped to the slight swell of her abdomen before returning to her pink-tinged face.

She gave him a blistering look. 'You think I would consent to making the same mistake twice?'

He had the gall to smile at her. 'I think it wouldn't take too much of an effort to get you to do so.'

She clenched her fists by her sides to stop herself from lifting one to the side of his arrogant face.

'I'd like to see you try,' she bit out furiously.

'Is that an invitation?' He closed the short distance between them, effectively trapping her between a full-sized marble statue and the hall table. 'I know I promised not to, but if you've changed your mind?'

'Don't touch me, Xavier.' Her voice sounded rusty and out of use and not half as insistent as she'd intended.

'You're the only person I know who can say one thing with their mouth while their eyes communicate something completely different,' he mused as he lifted a hand to her hair, trailing his fingers through the silky strands so gently she could scarcely breathe.

'You're imagining it,' she croaked.

'You keep giving me that look,' he said. 'And you know I can't resist that look.'

'W…what look?' She tried to pull away but he still had her tethered to him by a single tendril of her hair.

'That come-and-get-me look,' he said, releasing her hair to concentrate his gaze on her mouth. 'And then your lips go all soft and tremble slightly as if you can already feel my mouth on them.'

'I do no such thing!' she insisted, trying to clamp her lips together and speak at the same time.

He gave a soft chuckle of amusement. 'Stop fighting it,

Carli. What's the point in struggling against what is really inevitable?'

'Please, Xavier…' She didn't know what she was asking for, the words just slipping past the guard of her lips as if they had a mind of their own. 'Please…'

# CHAPTER SIX

XAVIER pressed a barely there kiss to the side of her mouth and she sucked in a prickly breath. He moved down to the jut of her bottom lip and took it between his warm lips, holding her captive with bone-melting tenderness.

She felt desire leap inside her like a forest fire, its hot tongues of need consuming all of her determination to resist him. He released her lip and pressed his mouth over hers, the smooth slide of his tongue into her mouth destroying all of her plans to push him away.

She felt the wall at her back and his hard body at her front, his masculine shape leaving her in no doubt of his arousal. The swell of her tummy between them only seemed to heighten her need to get closer to him, and the arms she'd pinned to her sides earlier now lifted to link around his neck, her fingers already threading their way through his thick dark hair.

He deepened the kiss even further, leaving her breathless as he pressed against her, his body searching for hers with burning intent. She felt his hand at her breast, his fingers gentle over her swollen tenderness, his lazy thumb rolling over her taut nipple, sending waves of desire to her quivering core.

His mouth left hers to trail a hot blaze from her neck, down over the smooth swell of her *décolletage,* his tongue dipping tantalisingly into the shadow between her breasts. When his mouth closed over her nipple she felt the graze of his teeth through the fabric of her blouse, and then as he lifted his head she saw the dampness of his mouth-print and the nectar of her need spilled inside her, melting her from the inside out.

As he lifted her into his arms she knew she should be making some sort of protest but the words didn't make it through the scrambled disorder of her desire-enfeebled brain. Her body was on automatic drive, its course set so determinedly there was nothing she could do to turn it about.

He carried her effortlessly upstairs and his mouth was still on hers as he laid her on his bed, his weight over her a delicious pressure as he positioned himself between her spreading thighs.

With an orchestration of movement which had its choreography set in the past he removed her clothes while her trembling fingers dealt with his. Her fingertips fluttered over his maleness and she heard him draw in a harsh breath as she revisited his pleasure points time and time again.

She let her hand fall away and slid down the bed to take him in her mouth, delighting in the flinch of his body as she captured him, his hands clawing through her hair, looking for an anchor against the spiralling pleasure she was giving him. She gloried in the power she had over him, his strength and potency totally under her control as he struggled to hold back his response to the ministrations of her lips and tongue.

At last he could stand no more and, hauling her upwards, claimed her mouth once more, pressing her back into the mattress with the urgency of his desire burning into her where his skin brushed along hers.

She was aflame with her need of him, each and every pore of her skin lifting as if to draw him closer. Her breasts were swollen against his chest, the masculine hairs of his body tickling her flesh from chest to thigh.

His hand slid down over the mound of her belly, his

fingers splayed in a touch of such poignant intimacy she felt tears prickling at the backs of her eyes. Their baby lay beneath his warm hand, its tiny body still too small to feel, but knowing it was there made her feel closer to Xavier in spite of all that had passed between them.

'I don't want to hurt you,' he breathed against her mouth as he raised his head to look down at her, his dark eyes glazed with passion.

'You won't hurt me,' she whispered back.

'I won't go too deep.' He moved against her carefully, his movements controlled and steady.

'I want to feel you…' She sighed with pleasure at the glide of his hard body, her body shivering in reaction to his gentle possession.

She felt him check himself before going deeper, the deepening thrust causing her body to grasp him tightly in remembered pleasure.

It felt so right to have him there. He filled her so completely, her body welcoming him as if he were returning home after a long absence.

He set a leisurely rhythm which was far too slow for her heightened state of arousal. She arched her back to bring him closer to where she wanted him but it still wasn't enough. She was close to begging when he slipped a hand between their straining bodies and sought the tiny pearl of her desire with devastating accuracy. She leapt at his touch, all the muscles in her body tensing in preparation for the final plunge into paradise.

Suddenly she was there, tipping over the edge of reason into a free-fall of ecstasy where no conscious thought belonged.

She floated back down to reality in time to feel his release pumping with gentle restraint into her still quivering body, his hectic breathing the only clue of how complete his pleasure had been.

It was only as the tide of passion ebbed that she realised how seriously she'd betrayed herself. She had done it again, allowed herself to be used by him when she'd promised herself she wouldn't. He'd only done it to prove how weak she was where he was concerned. Her reaction to him fuelled his male pride and he'd gone in search of it deliberately. She could barely look at him in case he saw the shame she felt written all over her body, let alone on her face.

She eased herself away from him and, gathering what dignity she could, scrambled to her feet and began hunting for her clothes, her emotions in such disarray she could barely get her fingers to respond to the task of picking her skirt up off the floor.

Xavier leaned up on one elbow to watch her, a small smile lurking about the corners of his mouth.

'What's the hurry, Carli?' he asked.

She turned her back and stepped into her skirt and dragged up the zip, muttering a single unprintable word as it snagged and caught on a loose thread.

'Come here and I'll help you,' he offered.

She gave the zip an almighty tug and freed it. 'No, thank you.'

'What's the matter?' he asked.

'How can you ask that?' She rounded on him furiously.

He gave her a guileless look as he linked his arms above his head. 'Are you ashamed of how you respond to me?'

'Of course I'm ashamed!' She thrust her arms through the sleeves of her blouse and began haphazardly rebuttoning it. 'We're not married any more and…and…'

'And we're expecting a baby,' he put in.

'And we hate each other!' She ignored his insert. 'It's not right! It's…it's…'

'It's natural.'

'It's not natural!' she insisted. 'You don't feel anything for me other than the most basic animal lust and I don't…'

'Don't what, Carli?'

She bit her lip and turned away to hunt for her shoes. 'I don't want to discuss this any more. You had no right to…to seduce me. You promised you wouldn't.'

'Whoa there for a minute.' He eased himself upright and came to stand in front of her. 'What's this talk of seducing? Who had their mouth around my—?'

'Stop it!' She pushed against his chest to prevent him from speaking her shame out loud. 'I'm not myself. I wasn't thinking.'

'To be perfectly frank, I prefer it when you don't think,' he said with a wry twist to his lips. 'When you think you start pulling away from me like you're doing right now. A few minutes ago you were begging me to—'

'Don't say it!' She spun away. 'Don't make me feel any worse.'

'What is it with you?' he asked in a frustrated tone. 'Isn't it a bit late for the outraged-virgin routine?'

She turned back to glare at him. 'How can you use me in such a way?'

He frowned heavily. 'I did not use you, Carli.'

'You only made love with me to prove a point.'

'You could have stopped me at any stage.'

'How could I?' She twisted her hands in front of her. 'I can't think straight when you touch me.'

'That's what you hate the most, isn't it, the fact that you can't stop yourself from responding to me?'

She turned away from his assessing look and folded her

arms across her chest protectively, wishing she hadn't been quite so unguarded with her tongue.

'Why is your need of me so threatening to you?' he asked.

'I do not need you,' she bit out. 'You caught me at a weak moment, that's all. I won't be such a pushover next time.'

'I never said you were.'

'You didn't have to.'

'You seem to have this goal in life to push everyone away in case they get too close. Why do you do that?' he asked. 'Is it something to do with your parents?'

'I don't want to talk about it.'

'At some point you're going to have to face the issues you brought to our marriage. You keep throwing the blame for our break-up in my face but I'm beginning to wonder now if that's only half of the story.'

'Our marriage broke up because you put your career ahead of it.'

'Either you tell me about your family, Carli, or I will take steps to find out for myself.'

'Go right ahead,' she said.

'Why won't you tell me?'

'Why won't you back off?' She glowered at him.

'What are you hiding?'

'Nothing.'

'Look, Carli, no one's family is perfect.'

'Yours claims to be.'

'My family is far from perfect,' he said heavily, 'even though it's taken me a long time to realise it. I thought the other night demonstrated that in ways words never could.'

Something in his tone drew her gaze back to his. And before she could stop herself, she took an unsteady breath and began to speak in a flat, emotionless tone. 'My father left my mother when I was ten. Apparently he'd fallen in love or lust with his young secretary. My mother was devastated and became increasingly depressed over the years.' She took another shaky breath and continued, 'When I was sixteen I came back from school camp to find her lying in the bath, her wrists slashed to the bone. I kept thinking if only I hadn't had that milkshake with my friends I might have found her in time. End of story.'

Xavier swallowed, his gut twisting painfully. 'You should've told me.'

'Why?' She gave him a chilly glance.

'I was your husband; I should've known about what you'd been through.'

'I don't like people feeling sorry for me. I had years of it. *"There goes the poor girl whose mother committed suicide."* Do you know what that feels like? To be stared at, wondered about, speculated on?'

'Have you told anyone?' he asked. 'Eliza, for instance?'

She shook her head, the line of her mouth grim. 'I met Eliza at university. After what I'd been through at school I decided to keep my past life totally private.'

'It must have been a nightmare.' His tone was gentle.

'It was but I'm over it now.'

'Are you?'

She shifted her eyes from his. 'I don't even think about it any more.'

'What about your father?' he asked. 'Have you seen him since your mother's death?'

'No and I don't want to.' Her voice was determined. 'He didn't just leave my mother, he left me as well.'

Xavier pressed his lips together in a musing gesture. 'I think I'm starting to see why our marriage was doomed to fail.'

'What do you mean?' She gave him a wary look.

'Your feelings of insecurity left little room for trust in our relationship. Your father abandoned your mother and as a result you see all men in much the same light, as unprincipled opportunists intent on riding roughshod over you to get what they want.'

'So it was my fault our marriage failed? What about your part in it?'

'I didn't say it was all your fault. However, if I had known how you had felt at the time, I could've made some allowances.'

'Such as?'

'I'm not sure,' he sighed. 'Maybe listen more. I seem to remember I wasn't all that good at that back then.'

She found his unexpected confession surprising, but instead of telling him so, remained silent.

'I guess I was so blinded by what I felt for you I couldn't see what was happening to us. And as you've said on previous occasions I was too career-focused. I had a goal in front of me and was heading straight for it; the fact that you were in the way of it didn't occur to me until it was too late. Like you, I was operating from the model set down by my family. I didn't question it; I just got on with it.'

'We both made mistakes.' She found her voice at last.

'I suppose the trick is not to make them again,' he said.

'Yes…' She lowered her gaze to stare at her hands.

He stood watching her for a moment, his forehead creased in a frown. It shocked him to think he'd been married to her for three years and in all that time he'd never known about the circumstances of her mother's death. He'd asked about her parents once or twice, but sensing her reluctance, had assumed she was slightly ashamed of her poorer background. He hadn't pressed her and had been content to simply fall into bed with her instead, not realising until now what a mistake it had been to let those sorts of sleeping dogs lie for so long.

No wonder she'd found their marriage so suffocating, not to mention his overbearing family. Her fight for independence had been more of a fight for survival because she never wanted to be as vulnerable as her mother had been. Her career had been her passport to the sort of financial freedom her mother had had no access to and in his ignorance he had expected her to relinquish that security.

'Carli…' He swallowed, wondering where he should begin, but she'd already gone to the door and was opening it.

'I need some time alone,' she said without turning to look at him.

It was the slap in the face he knew he deserved but it stung all the same.

'I understand.'

The door closed behind her but Xavier knew it would be hours, maybe even days before the fragrance of her perfume left his room.

# CHAPTER SEVEN

CARLI waited until Xavier had left the house the next morning before coming downstairs. She knew she was being a coward but every time she thought of how she'd responded to him the night before she felt herself grow hot inside out with shame.

How could she have let him win another round? It meant nothing to him, it was just sex, but to her it was everything. She hadn't just given him her body; she'd offered him her soul, but he'd trampled on it just as her father had done to her mother, just as Aidan Dangar was doing to Eliza.

Her visit to her friend later that afternoon was hardly reassuring.

'What do you mean you didn't go to the doctor?' Carli asked as she picked up the squawking baby off the floor. 'You promised me you'd go.'

Eliza gave her a sullen look and reached for her cigarettes. 'I forgot.'

'How could you forget? I phoned you an hour before to remind you.'

'I changed my mind.'

'Eliza, this is ridiculous. You want to keep the children, don't you?'

'You know I do.'

'Then this is where the battle begins, can't you see that?' Carli urged. 'You have to be healthy, it's a major priority. No court will hand you full custody of the kids unless you can prove you're up to the task of taking care of them.'

121

'Trust you to take Xavier's side in this. What did he do to get you on side? Coax you back into his bed?'

Carli could feel her guilt wash over her face but there was nothing she could do to stop it.

Eliza gave her a sneering look. 'I thought as much. You never could resist him, could you?'

'My relationship with Xavier is not open for discussion,' she said firmly. 'What we're discussing here is your health. I'm going to call the doctor's surgery right now and arrange an immediate appointment and I will accompany you. I don't care if I have to drag you kicking and screaming from this house, you're coming with me and that's that.'

Eliza gave in with bad grace but Carli felt grateful that at least when they left the house half an hour later it was only baby Brody who'd done the kicking and screaming.

She sat in the waiting room while Eliza saw the doctor, the baby chewing messily on a teething rusk as he sat on her lap. Four-year-old Amelia sat at her feet playing with a puzzle with the sort of quiet intent that secretly worried Carli. How many of her parents' arguments had the solemn little girl overheard? What fears did that small blonde head contain?

Eliza came out of the doctor's surgery with a blood-sample patch on one arm and a watery smile on her face.

'What did she say?' Carli asked softly as they walked out to the car, conscious of Amelia's acute hearing.

'You were right, Carli. The doctor thinks I've got a hormone imbalance. She took some blood and though it will take a couple of days to know for certain she's confident that what I've got is an autoimmune disease called Grave's disease. I know the name isn't all that reassuring but apparently it's quite common after pregnancy and certainly all my symptoms fit.'

'How do they treat it?'

'Tablets, or sometimes an operation to remove part of the thyroid gland.'

'You'll have to tell Aidan straight away,' Carli insisted. 'He needs to know.'

Eliza gave her a quelling look as she got into the car. 'To borrow one of your own phrases of five years ago: I'm never going to see or speak to my husband ever again.'

Carli clipped Amelia's seat belt into place without responding; there were far too many of her phrases from the past coming back to haunt her without Eliza adding to their number.

As the rest of the week unfolded Carli became increasingly aware of Xavier's efforts to keep his distance. He addressed her both politely and briefly in the mornings but she spent the evenings alone, usually going to bed before he came home.

She lay in bed each night listening to the sounds of him moving about the house, wishing she had the courage to face him and tell him of her regrets over what had happened in the past.

Whenever she heard the sound of his firm tread on the stairs she couldn't help holding her breath until they went past her door to the master bedroom further down the hall.

Every night when she heard the shower running in the bathroom she tortured herself with images of his hard-muscled body standing beneath the spray, her hands clenching into fists either side of her to stop them from twitching the bedcovers aside so she could join him as she had done so many times when they'd been together.

It didn't make for a restful night and the long, empty days were no better. Without the structure of work she grew increasingly restless, her nerves stretching to breaking point as she imagined Xavier out each night with another woman. Why else would he be out so late every evening?

On Friday evening, rather than sit waiting in an empty house, Carli took herself to a movie, not bothering to leave a message on Xavier's answering service as he hadn't been home before eleven all week.

She sat in the almost empty row and stared at the screen but her thoughts kept drifting until she lost track of the complicated plot. The images flickered anonymously as she thought about her future with Xavier, unable to stop herself from agonising over what might have been.

How different it would be if they were looking forward to a life together with their expected child as a bonus! How different if would be if love was what bound them, not responsibility.

Just as she was about to leave the cinema she felt a tiny fluttering in her belly and stood very still, waiting to see if she would feel it again. She held her breath and another flutter started, the tiny movement reminding her of the wings of a tiny moth trapped inside someone's gently closed palm.

She smiled a soft smile as her hand rested on her abdomen, a great wave of love for Xavier coursing through her as she thought of their tiny infant stretching its limbs inside her.

She had only just turned her key in the lock on returning to his house when the door was flung open to reveal Xavier standing over her in a towering rage.

'I suppose it might be too much to ask where you have been for the last—' he inspected his watch '—five or so hours?'

She brushed past him in the doorway and, dropping her

bag to the floor, turned and faced him. 'I wasn't aware I had to sign in and sign out.'

'Where have you been?' he growled at her. 'I've been out of my mind with worry.'

She gave him a cynical glance. 'Why don't you qualify that statement? You were worried about the baby—not me.'

He frowned at her tone. 'I called your office and they told me you were on two weeks' sick leave. How could you think I wasn't worried about you?'

'Your concern is really rather touching but completely wasted on me,' she said. 'I was out. That's all you need to know.'

'With whom?'

'I could ask you the very same question for every night of this past week but I'm not going to pretend an interest I don't feel.'

'What's that supposed to mean?'

She gave him a withering look. 'You've got a hide, hauling me over the coals for deigning to come here at—' she inspected her watch as he had done '—ten-thirty when every night this week you haven't come in before eleven.'

'I was working.'

'At what?' she asked. 'Your love life?'

'That's a reprehensible thing to say, considering our current relationship.'

'And just what is our current relationship?' She sent him a black look. 'Why don't you run it past me one more time? I'm a little hazy on the particulars.'

'You know exactly what it is.'

'Let me remember, now…oh, yes, it's all coming back to me now. You got me pregnant and you're doing the right thing by me by insisting I live with you, blackmail being your *modus operandi*. How could I forget?'

'You're being totally unreasonable.'

'*I'm* being unreasonable?'

'I'm trying to do the right thing by you.'

'The right thing?' She glared at him furiously. 'The right thing would have been to leave me alone in the first place.'

He folded his arms across his chest and adopted a pose of extreme boredom. 'OK, I can see you're itching for a showdown so let's get it over with.'

She was incensed by his attitude. 'I can't believe your two-faced audacity! I have spent every night this week in solitude, I go out just once to a movie and you're calling in the FBI to track my movements. What sort of double standard is that?'

'What movie did you see?'

'It was…' She hunted through her brain for a title but it came up with nothing; she couldn't even recall a principal actor. 'I don't remember. I wasn't all that interested.'

The look he gave her was cynical. 'Nice try, but wholly unconvincing.'

'I did see a movie!'

'Yeah, right.'

'I'm not good with titles when I'm stressed.'

'I believe you,' he said in a tone which suggested he didn't.

'I was distracted…I didn't follow the plot.'

'Now you're getting desperate.'

She felt like screaming at him. 'I was thinking about other things!'

'What other things?'

'What's with all these questions?' she asked. 'Why don't you tell me where you were all this week?'

'Why didn't you tell me you weren't going in to work?' he threw back.

'You're never home long enough to talk about anything,' she said.

'Have you missed me?'

'Of course I didn't miss you!'

'Then why ask me where I've been?'

'I…' She floundered for a moment. 'I don't see why I have to reveal all my movements to you if you don't do the same for me.'

'I already told you—I was at work. If you don't believe me you can always check with my secretary.'

'She'd only say what you pay her to say,' she shot back cynically.

'I think you do Elaine a disservice,' he said. 'Like you, she thinks I'm a total jerk for how I've treated you in the past.'

She stared at him, her anger fading as if he'd flicked a switch.

'She…she does?'

'She thinks you're far too sweet for me,' he said, his expression wry. 'Mind you, I didn't let on about the vases. I thought she might see that for herself the next time you come into my office in one of your fight-picking moods.'

'Very funny,' she drawled. 'Why don't you nail down the furniture in case I'm tempted to add a filing cabinet to my repertoire?'

He held her defiant look with lazy amusement. 'Somehow I can't quite see you tossing anything bigger than a pot plant at me in your condition.' His eyes slid over the tight mound of her abdomen before returning to her caramel gaze.

Carli felt heat coursing through her at his lazy appraisal, her skin lifting in sharp awareness of him standing so close to her.

She moistened her dry lips and made to step back but one of his hands came down on her shoulder in a warm touch that sent a shiver of reaction to her toes and back.

'Don't run away, Carli.'

'I…I'm not running away…'

His eyes held the nervous flicker of hers. 'I want to feel my baby growing inside you.'

Her eyes widened as his hand slid from her shoulder to the mound of her belly, his long fingers pressing over her with exploratory gentleness.

She saw his expression change from seriousness to wonder. 'Can you feel anything?' he asked.

'I can feel your hand.'

'I meant the baby. Can you feel it moving yet?'

'I felt it this evening for the first time,' she said, her tone instantly softening. 'It was faint at first but the second time was stronger.'

He moved his hand over her in a caressing motion, sending her pulses soaring as his fingers sought the overstrained fastening of her skirt.

'Do you mind?' he asked, hesitating.

She shook her head, not trusting herself to speak, her breath locking in the back of her throat at the feel of his warm hand on her bare flesh.

'Do you ever wonder what the baby will look like?' he asked after a moment.

'Yes…'

'So do I,' he confessed. 'I keep imagining a little girl with curly chestnut hair and a fiery temper.'

'I've been thinking along the lines of a boy with black hair and an arrogant disposition.'

He grinned down at her as he removed his hand. 'I wonder who'll be right.'

She adjusted her skirt with suddenly uncooperative fingers. 'I don't really care as long as he or she arrives safely.'

'Are you worried about the birth?' he asked.

'A bit…' She caught her lip between her teeth. 'It's times like this that I really miss my mother.'

Xavier frowned at the inherent sadness in her tone. It was one of the first times he had heard her mention her mother voluntarily and he wondered if it meant she was starting to trust him.

'I'll be there for you,' he said.

She gave him a sceptical look. 'Yes, but for how long?'

'What do you mean for how long?' he asked. 'You know how much I want this baby.'

'The baby, yes.'

'You think I don't want you as well?'

She gave him a twisted, humourless smile. 'I'm not exactly the woman of your choice, am I?'

His frown deepened at the hint of regret in her tone. 'Carli…' He paused, searching for the right words.

'Don't insult me by pretending you want me as well as the baby,' she got in before he could speak. 'I know what your plan will be as soon as it's born.'

'Then perhaps you'll be so kind as to enlighten me, as I haven't the faintest idea of what you're talking about.'

She threw him a derisory glance. 'How long will it be before you make your move to snatch my baby away from me?'

'You think I would do that?'

'Wouldn't you?'

'Of course I wouldn't.'

'You do it for others,' she said. 'How is Aidan Dangar, by the way? Have you two been busily planning the annihilation of Eliza all week?'

'Look, I know what sort of reputation I have and for the most part it's warranted,' he said. 'I confess ever since our divorce I have been somewhat heavy-handed in cases where I considered there to be a grasping ex-wife who wanted to twist the knife a little bit.'

'You think *I* was like that towards you?' she asked. 'I didn't ask for a whopping settlement. I could have but I didn't.'

'No, perhaps not, but you can hardly deny your bitterness towards me,' he said. 'You constantly made things difficult as the papers were being processed.'

If only he knew why she had been deliberately obstructive, she thought sadly.

'If I was bitter you have only yourself to blame,' she said. 'I gave our marriage everything I could, including letting my career slip to make room for yours. But in the end there was nothing left for me to do but get out before I ended up like my mother.'

'Your mother's situation was completely different. You didn't have to throw away what we had. We could've worked it out.'

'How?' she asked. 'By me subsuming my life into yours as your mother did for your father? I would've gone mad getting my hair done twice a week and going to numerous bridge and sherry parties.'

'My mother is of a different generation, but you could have carved your own way.'

'How? By having the brood of children you expected me to deliver in rapid succession?'

'I only suggested starting a family because I thought it might help you to feel more settled. I was getting desperate. I didn't want to lose you.'

'You didn't fight the divorce.'

'Yeah, well, male pride has its limits, you know.' He turned away to make his way up the stairs. 'I'm going to have a shower. Mrs Fingleton left something in the oven for dinner. Help yourself.'

She sighed as she watched him go up the stairs, wishing she could find the words to call him back.

He'd loved her once; could he do so again?

Carli woke after a fitful sleep to hear Xavier moving about downstairs. She tossed back the bedcovers and, slipping on a light robe, made her way down to the kitchen.

He turned to look at her as she came in, taking in her tousled hair and hollow eyes with a sweeping glance.

'Bad night?' he guessed, handing her a cup.

She took the cup and, dragging out a chair, sat down. 'I think it's the strange bed. I can't seem to get used to it.'

He leant back against the bench, one ankle crossed over the other in a casual pose. 'Why not move back into mine?'

Her eyes skittered away from his as she cradled the cup in her hands. 'I don't think that's such a good idea.'

'Why not?'

'You know why not.'

'Because you don't want to admit to wanting me?'

'No…I mean yes…NO!'

'You sound confused.' His tone was light with amusement.

'I'm not confused. I just don't want to complicate things any further. We've been divorced for five years, how can you expect me to slip back into bed with you as if nothing has happened?'

'How will it complicate things if we conduct a normal relationship?'

'Normal?' she blurted. 'What exactly is normal about this situation between us?'

'You're making things more difficult than they need to be,' he said. 'We could have a very satisfactory relationship if only you'd let go of your anger towards me.'

'Satisfactory for whom?'

'For both of us,' he said.

'How long do you expect such a relationship to last?' she asked. 'One of us might fall in love. What then?'

He turned to put his cup in the sink before he answered. 'I guess if our emotions were engaged elsewhere it could prove difficult, but I have no such engagement at this point, and you clearly don't, otherwise you wouldn't be pregnant to me, so it's a moot point.'

'I wouldn't be pregnant to you if you hadn't made it impossible for me to say no.'

'You like that high horse of yours, don't you?' He gave her a mocking smile. 'If it appeases your conscience to paint me as the dark seducer who had his wicked way with you, go right ahead; it doesn't really concern me. You came to me willingly, perhaps more willingly than any other woman I've had in the past five years.'

Carli's hand around her empty cup tightened until her knuckles were as white as her set mouth, rage boiling in her blood until she could hardly see out of her flashing eyes.

'If you're going to throw that cup at me let me warn you, pregnant or not, there will be consequences,' he warned her, his words so closely echoing those of the past it triggered the flickering pulse of expectation between her thighs.

She didn't give a damn about the consequences. She clenched her teeth and threw the cup but he raised his hand and caught it mid-air, placing it on the bench with a nerve-jangling chink as his steely gaze collided with hers.

'There's a whole tea service in the cupboard to the left of you,' he said. 'But why not help yourself to the Wedgwood on the right?'

'You don't know how tempted I am to do exactly that,' she spat back.

'Don't let me spoil your fun. I'm more than happy to wait for mine.'

The sensation between her thighs flickered again, more strongly this time.

'What are you going to do, Xavier?' she goaded with a courage she didn't quite feel. 'Force yourself on me?'

His eyes held hers for a tense pause. Carli wished she hadn't thrown the words at him, for she knew if he took it into his head to prove his point she would have no defence. She wanted him as much if not more than he wanted her and she was sure he knew it.

'You know me better than that, Carli,' he said in a voice deep and rough with desire. 'One kiss is all it would take and we'd both go up in flames.'

Carli felt the heat rising in her traitorous body, making her limbs weaken with need. She saw the answering blaze of passion in his dark gaze as it ran over her lightly, lingering on the swell of her breasts before returning to her flushed features.

'Want to put it to the test?' he asked, stepping closer, his chest almost brushing the pointed, aching peaks of her breasts.

She couldn't breathe. Her body was leaning towards him without her permission, the words of resistance locked somewhere in the back of her throat.

'One kiss, Carli…' His warm breath feathered the upper curve of her mouth, making her lips tingle with the need to feel his mouth on hers. 'Just one little kiss…'

Her eyelids came down in time with his lowering mouth, the air of her escaping sigh mingling intimately with his breath. She felt the stroke of his tongue and her mouth flowered open beneath the increasing pressure of his as he took possession. She felt the hard planes and ridges of his body against the soft pliancy of hers, increasing her desire for his commanding, intimate presence.

He lifted his mouth from hers and she felt the burr of his skin along the sensitive curve of her cheek as he trailed a hot blaze of kisses over her face, each one leaving her breathless with clawing, grasping need.

His mouth returned to hers with renewed purpose, drawing from her a response she had previously fought with herself not to give, but she knew now it was hopeless. She wanted his kisses, his caresses and his possession and there seemed no point denying it any longer. Holding him off was punishing her, not him. He could always find someone else but she had only ever wanted him.

Five years apart had changed nothing.

What did it matter if he felt nothing for her any more? She was carrying his child, so surely that counted for something?

It *had* to count for something.

She drew in a ragged breath as he parted her robe, the solid press of his body against hers thrilling her in breathless anticipation. She felt his hand searching for the betrayal of her neediness, the silky slide of his long fingers inside her, sucking the air right out of her chest. He played her like an instrument, the music of his caress rising in a crescendo in her body. She felt the tightening of her inner muscles, the hectic pulse of her blood asking, pleading for more and more of his expert touch. She felt herself soaring and choked out a gasp of surprise as her body clutched at his fingers greedily, her back arching so she could extend the pleasure for as long as she could.

She heard the rasp of his zip but hardly registered it had been her hand that had released it. She heard the swift inward draw of his breath as her fingers feathered over him, lingering on the already moistened tip, the strong surge of blood thickening him even further as she stroked and caressed him.

'You're going to have to stop that,' he gave a rough gasp, 'or in about sixty seconds you're going to get more than you bargained for.'

She increased her pressure subtly, knowing exactly what would send him over the edge. How many times had she done this in the past? She had delighted in it, relishing in the feeling of feminine power it gave her to know she could bring him to a quivering, shuddering release with the touch of her mouth or hands.

'You want me to stop?' she asked, deliberately slowing down the movement of her hand.

His dark eyes glittered with unrelieved tension, burning a pathway to her soul as they seared hers. '*No…*' he groaned, bracing himself.

She gave him a look from beneath her lashes and shimmied down his body until she was on her knees before him.

'Oh, my God…'

She smiled around him, her teeth scraping him gently, teasingly, just the way he liked it. He looked down at her and wondered if he was dreaming. How many times had they done this in the past?

He felt himself going over the edge and there was nothing he could do to stop it. He shut his eyes and let himself go…

Carli got to her feet and turned away, not sure she wanted him to see how much his response had affected her. It seemed so ironical that she could taste him in her mouth and yet she didn't even know what he thought about her now. Did he still hate her for insisting on a divorce after that final argument? He had every right to, for she had acted so childishly when all it would have taken to repair things was a simple 'I'm sorry'. Her pride way back then hadn't been too heavily into those two words and nor indeed had his. Hadn't the passage of time changed anything between them?

She suddenly felt cold in spite of the summer temperature, her body feeling feeble and unsupported without the hard presence of his against hers.

He seemed uncomfortable meeting her gaze and she watched as he moved away towards the pantry, tossing over his shoulder with enviable casualness, 'Want some breakfast?'

She stared at him, wondering how he could possibly think of food at a time like this.

'What's wrong?' he asked, turning back to face her, his expression giving no hint of what had so recently passed between them.

It irritated her that he could be so unaffected while she was still struggling to quell the aftershocks of his touch on her tender flesh.

'No, thanks,' she said with deliberate irony. 'I've already had something.'

He gave her a droll look as he reached for the cereal. 'Very funny.'

She stood uncertainly before him, trying to decode his mood, but he was as inscrutable as ever. She gave herself a mental shake and forced her mouth into speech, saying the first thing that came into her head. 'I was just wondering what you do on the weekends these days. Since it's Saturday I thought you might have something in mind.'

He tipped some cereal into a bowl before answering. 'I do.' He poured some milk over the cereal and placed the carton back on the bench, his gaze deliberately meeting and holding hers. 'I'm playing golf with Aidan Dangar.'

It wasn't quite the answer she'd been expecting, nor was it particularly heartening to think of him spending three hours with Eliza's soon-to-be ex-husband, no doubt formulating the removal of the children from her custody as soon as he possibly could.

'So while he's busy chasing stupid little white balls around an overgrown lawn with you, what do you expect his sick wife to be doing?' she asked, unable to stop the resentful pitch of her voice in time.

'And the point of your question is?'

'He should be at home helping Eliza get better, not sucking up to you so you can help him take her to the cleaners.'

'I take it you've been listening to her well-worn sob story of how hard life is in the suburbs.'

She took immediate offence at his sneering tone. 'She's not well, Xavier. She's got a hormone imbalance.'

'She's a complete nutter, that's what she is,' he tossed back. 'Have you been to the house lately? Surely you don't think the way she lives is normal? I don't blame Aidan for escaping that hell hole.'

'How absolutely typical!' she snorted. 'You don't get it, do you? You men are all the same. You expect the women in your life to look like a supermodel and cook like a celebrity chef and yet as soon as the relationship hits a rough patch you're out of there with the divorce papers flapping in your wake.'

'If you remember, you were the one who insisted on a divorce, not me,' he reminded her.

'We're not discussing us, we're discussing Eliza and Aidan!' she said heatedly.

'Stay out of it, Carli,' he cautioned. 'Eliza's been running off the rails for months.'

'You're not listening to me,' she said in frustration. 'Eliza is unwell. Once she gets better hopefully so too will their relationship.'

'You're a lawyer, not a marriage counsellor. Besides,

shouldn't you be concentrating on what's happening in your own life before you take on someone else's problems?'

She felt her shoulders sag with the effort of holding her fort against him. 'I just wish you wouldn't dismiss my opinions as if they don't count. I hate it when you do that.'

'Sweetheart, listen to me.' He hitched up her chin with a long, tanned finger as her heart tripped over itself at the first endearment he'd used in five long years. His eyes held hers with mesmerising force, her breathing becoming shallow and erratic as he drew her closer, almost touching but not quite. She felt the magnetic pull of his body and had to do everything in her power to resist it.

'I'm very interested in your opinions and if I had more time right now there are a few I'd like a little more information on, but I promised Aidan I'd spend the morning with him. He's not handling this situation all that well.'

'Tell him not to go through with the divorce,' she said, pulling out of his embrace.

'It's not my place to tell him how to run his life.'

'He'll destroy Eliza if he goes through with it,' she said. 'I just know he will.'

He gave her a long, hard look that made her feel increasingly uneasy. She'd never been all that comfortable with his dark scrutiny and now even less so. She hardly realised she was holding her breath until he spoke, his deep, velvety voice forcing the banked up air in her lungs out in a rush that made her feel instantly light-headed.

'All right,' he said. 'I will talk to him but on one condition and one condition only.'

She gave a small swallow sigh, somehow knowing just where his incisive brain had led him. She'd practically handed the opportunity to him on a plate, which made her feel all the more angry, but with herself, not him.

She forced herself to hold his glittering gaze. 'I assume you've thought of another way to blackmail me into resuming a physical relationship with you,' she said through tight lips.

'You don't think that what happened here a few minutes ago isn't part of having a physical relationship?' he asked incredulously. 'Exactly what planet have you been living on in the last five years?'

Her eyes skittered away from his. 'It was a mistake…you made me angry and when I'm angry I don't think straight.'

'So what you're saying is: you don't want to have sex with me ever again, right?'

She straightened her spine and met his penetrating gaze. 'That's correct.'

'Liar, liar, pants on fire,' he teased, his dark eyes glinting. 'Come on, darling. You're giving me that look again so don't waste your breath on words that are meaningless.'

She could feel her insides melting with his second endearment, but there was no way she was going to openly agree to his bribe. What would be the point? She didn't need to be blackmailed into his bed. God help her, she wanted to be there—permanently.

She schooled her features into nonchalance and, turning aside, reached for a bowl and the cereal packet he'd left on the bench earlier. The sound of the grains and flakes of the muesli falling into the bowl sounded as loud as rain on a tin roof, so heavy was the silence.

'So you've decided you're hungry after all?' he mused.

'I'm thinking of the baby.'

'Good, now we're finally getting somewhere.' He reached for the carton of milk and held it out to her, his eyes holding hers. 'Want some?'

'Yes…thank you,' she said, unable to drag her eyes away.

He poured in a measure slowly, his eyes still fastened on hers. 'Enough?'

She nodded and he put the carton aside, still without letting her gaze go.

The silence pulsed for several heavy heartbeats.

Carli felt the flutter of her blood trying to get through to where it was supposed to go, felt too the hollowing of her stomach as he took the cereal bowl out of her hands and took just one small step towards her.

Xavier stared down at her uptilted face, wondering what was going on behind the screen of her caramel gaze.

There were times when he seriously wondered if she was starting to care for him once more. She responded to him physically without restraint, but then, he reminded himself, she had done so just as readily in the past, and, if his reputation over the last five years was anything to go by, she was by no means alone.

The trouble between them wasn't the sex. It was good if not better than before, and certainly a whole lot better than what he'd had since she'd left him, but still he felt as if something was missing.

He had loved her so deeply but their acrimonious divorce had made it turn sour and he hadn't wanted to let his guard slip since. But sometimes when he looked at her just like this, his eyes holding hers, he felt something stir deep inside him, like a gear trying to change before the clutch was pressed down properly.

He drew in a breath that seemed to snag at his chest on the way through and he stepped backwards to put some distance between them. He noticed her eyes immediately lost their guarded sheen, her whole body relaxing as if the fear of his touch had dissipated as soon as he'd stepped away.

It wasn't encouraging.

Disappointment filtered through him, making his voice sound hard and somewhat distant when he finally spoke. 'I should be home around two pm. I hope you can find something meaningful to do to fill in the time.'

Her chin came up a notch as she sent him a castigating glance. 'I think I might be just about able to cope with your absence, but please don't hurry home on my account.'

His mouth tightened momentarily. 'Perhaps then you'll be available to have dinner with me this evening?' He knew he sounded sarcastic but was unable to correct it in time.

She lowered her gaze and reached for her abandoned cereal and tipped it into the sink before turning back to face him. 'I'll let you know,' she said and before he could do or say anything to stop her she left the room.

Xavier looked at the soggy mess of her uneaten breakfast lying in the sink, the dark raisins staring back up at him like accusing eyes.

He let out one short, sharp swear word and, turning the tap on full, stood and waited until they disappeared down the drain.

# CHAPTER EIGHT

CARLI spent the morning by the pool in the garden, forcing herself to relax enough to enjoy the warm sunshine and refreshing water. She swam back and forth, remembering the way Xavier had often joined her in the past, his long strokes so much more efficient than hers when they had tried to race each other.

She stopped for a breather and gave a little sigh as she trailed her fingertips in the crystal-clear water in front of her. So much of what had constituted their relationship had been combative and competitive. She had fought with him rather than discussed things evenly and rationally, her immature temper tantrums gradually eroding his love away.

The worst of it was she hadn't even really meant it when she'd asked for a divorce. Her thoughts drifted to that night… She could still hear the sound of Xavier's strong, purposeful stride as he crunched over the broken porcelain on the floor…

The look in his eyes should have warned her she'd pushed him to the very limits of his patience. They were twin deep, dark blue pools of simmering anger as his fingers bit into the flesh of her upper arms to haul her up against him, his mouth burning hers with the duel flames of rage and unrestrained desire.

To her shame she hadn't been able to resist him. She had kissed him back just as savagely, her own desire leaping out of control as it always did as soon as he touched her. She tasted blood and had no idea if it was hers or his.

She didn't care. She wanted him to ache for her the way she ached for him. She wanted him weak and helpless with need the way he made her.

The hall table lamp tottered and fell to the floor as they shoved the table on their way past; their mouths locked together, their hands tearing at each other's clothes with no regard to their preservation.

They hadn't made love in over a week. Deep down she knew it was probably why she was feeling so neglected and insecure, frightened in case he didn't want her any more, but nothing in her nature would allow her to admit it to him. Instead she had chosen to goad him into being so angry with her, he lost control. And he was losing control—rapidly. His breathing was hard-pressed as he backed her up against the wall, his first rough thrust sending shock-waves of delight right through her. She clung to him unashamedly, her body tightening around him, her breath coming out in sharp little gasps as he increased his pace. The silky slide of his hardened flesh tipped her over into oblivion, her head spinning with the sensations flooding her system as she shook and quivered in the tight band of his arms.

He barely waited for her storm to be over before he came with a forceful surge, his deep, primal groan like music to her ears.

She opened her eyes to see him looking at her, his expression still dark with anger.

'Satisfied now?' he asked, his breathing not quite even. 'Isn't that what tonight's little routine was all about?'

She tried to step away but his arms had locked on to the wall either side of her head, effectively trapping her.

'Answer me, damn you!' he growled.

'No,' she denied vehemently.

'I don't believe you,' he said.

'I don't care.'

He gave her a flinty look. 'You know, Carli, you only have to ask the next time you want a quick—'

'I want a divorce,' she blurted to stop him from speaking the crude word out loud.

The sudden silence roared in her ears until she felt light-headed.

His eyes went almost black as he stepped back from her. She watched as he reached for his trousers, stepping into them with the sort of cold precision she had come to dread.

Oh, what had she done?

'Xavier…' She took a step towards him but stopped when she saw the derision in his eyes as they ran over her from head to foot.

She was aware of her partial nakedness and never in her whole time with him had she felt more ashamed. His scathing look had marked her as the trailer trash his sisters and parents had always assumed her to be.

'So you want a divorce, do you, Carli?' he asked, his tone containing just the right amount of scorn to push her back into her tight corner.

'That's what I said.' She lifted her chin defiantly. *But I didn't mean it!* she wanted to tack on, but her injured pride wouldn't permit it.

'Then you shall have one,' he said. 'Because believe me, I will do nothing to stop you.'

She wanted him to stop her. Why wasn't he stopping her?

She stared at him as he scooped up his wrecked shirt off the floor, his foot kicking the broken lamp out of his way as he made his way to the front door.

She watched in silence as he opened it, flinging one last, blistering look her way before he slammed it on his exit.

\*   \*   \*

Carli stared down at the circular motion of the water she'd disturbed with her fingers, the movement of the tiny circles into larger and larger ones reminding her of how her reckless words and actions had done far more damage than she'd ever expected. She had issued him with the divorce papers, never really expecting him to go through with it. Even as the papers were returned to her signed she could hardly believe it was his signature there, but it had been too late to erase it.

She left the pool and after a quick shower spent the rest of the afternoon away from the house, not wanting to give Xavier the impression she was languishing about waiting for his return.

She went into the city and wandered around the shops for hours, stopping once or twice to purchase an item or two for the baby. Her fingers lingered over the tiny garments as she inspected them, wondering what it would feel like to hold her baby for the very first time.

The baby stirred in her womb as she held up a newborn-sized blue matinée jacket and she wondered if she was carrying a boy. But then, just as her hand reached out for a pink babygro suit the baby wriggled again and she couldn't help a tiny smile.

She bought both.

Xavier paced the empty lounge and glared at the telephone each round he did as if his hard look would instantly cause it to ring.

It didn't.

His morning with Aidan hadn't been all that enjoyable. His friend hadn't had his eye on the ball once and had seemed to be in a hurry to end the game and move on. Xavier couldn't help wondering where he was rushing off to or to whom.

He'd tried bringing up the topic of Eliza's health but Aidan had skirted away from it, preferring to discuss the date of the divorce instead.

'I want to get out of my marriage and fast,' Aidan said, swinging his five iron somewhat recklessly.

Xavier waited until the ball had disappeared into the rough before responding. 'Why don't you take a back pedal for a while and see what gives?'

'You're going soft on me, Xavier.' Aidan's look was berating. 'I couldn't believe it when you pulled out of acting for me. I thought you were my mate.'

Xavier settled his five iron in place and took a practice swing. 'I told you why.' He took the final swing but it wasn't much better than Aidan's.

'Yeah, that ex-wife of yours has you under the thumb,' Aidan put in scathingly. 'What were you thinking to get involved with her again? She cut you up before; why go back for seconds?'

Xavier looked into the distance and found his ball lying in the bunker, his eyes squinting against the bright sunshine. 'You know how it is,' he said, 'old habits are hard to break.'

'Interesting choice of words,' Aidan said, giving him a direct look. 'Just how pregnant is she?'

Xavier shifted his gaze back to the plight of his ball in the distance. 'You of all people should know there are no degrees of pregnancy. It's a yes or no answer.'

Aidan gave him a rolled-eyed look. 'How many weeks?'

'We're measuring it in months now.' Xavier's glance was wry. 'Almost five, to be precise.'

Aidan let his breath out between his teeth as they walked on. 'You always were a little out of control where she was concerned, weren't you?'

Xavier didn't answer. His denial wasn't going to sound

any more convincing than his silence, and, as he wasn't prepared to admit how he felt about Carli even to himself, he didn't see why he should go into unnecessary detail now.

'You still feel anything for her?' Aidan asked after they'd covered another hundred metres of the fairway.

'I thought we were here to discuss your situation, not mine?' Xavier said, looking straight ahead.

'My situation is completely different,' Aidan said. 'As far as I see it, Carli is still the same old Carli. Eliza, however, is now someone else.'

Xavier frowned as he thought about his friend's statement. Was Carli the same as she'd been five or so years ago? Or had she changed? And if so, had it been him who had changed her?

On a last-minute impulse Carli booked in for a hair treatment in an effort to stall the act of her final capitulation to Xavier. She knew as soon as she went through the door of his house she was going to be his for as long as he wanted her. It didn't matter how hard she tried to resist him, or how fervently she issued warnings to herself about how she was going to get dreadfully hurt in the end, all she could think of was how much she loved him. He was as necessary to her as the air she drew into her lungs to inflate them. He filled her. He completed her in a way no one else could. Yes, they were different in every way possible, but wasn't that what created good chemistry? She felt only half alive when he wasn't sparring with her, his sharp intelligence keeping her dancing on her toes in a way no one had ever done before or since.

Once her hair was finished she lingered over a last-minute latte in a small, cosy café, her legs already starting to tingle at the thought of Xavier coming between them. She pressed them together underneath the café table, her cheeks growing hotter by the second as she pushed her half-finished coffee away.

Half an hour later she made her way to the front door of Xavier's house, but before she could locate her key the door opened and he stood there before her, his expression full of reproach.

'What is the point of having a mobile phone if you never have it switched on?' he asked.

Carli brushed past him in the doorway and placed her carrier bags on the hall table, taking her time to lay her keys and purse down side by side on the polished surface.

She could see his tall figure standing just behind her in the gilt-edged mirror, his dark blue gaze fixed on her.

'I asked you a question.'

She turned around to face him. 'Did you tell Aidan to call off the divorce?'

He held her direct look for a moment without responding.

'I asked you a question.' She used the same curt tone he'd used earlier, folding her arms across her chest just as he had done.

'I did raise the topic but he seemed disinclined to talk about it. I guess he thinks it's none of my business now I'm not acting for him.'

She gave him a searching look as her arms dropped back by her sides. 'You've really dropped the case?'

He tilted one eyebrow ironically. 'Isn't that what you asked me to do?'

'Yes…'

'But you didn't think I was going to do it, did you?'

'I wasn't sure…'

'What would it take to get you to trust me?' he asked.

'I don't know…' She caught her lip, her eyes moving away from his.

'I handed the case to someone else in the firm. Aidan wasn't all that happy about it, of course.'

'What did you tell him?' she asked, fiddling with the strap of her watch to avoid his all-seeing gaze.

'Not much,' he said. 'He knew I was seeing you again so I guess he put two and two together.'

Seeing each other again... How casual that sounded, she thought sadly.

'What did you buy?' Xavier changed the subject as his glance fell upon the bags she'd placed on the hall table earlier.

'A few things for the baby,' she told him.

'Show me.'

She went to the first bag and held up the blue matinée jacket.

'Cute.' He smiled down at her. 'So you think it's a boy?'

She went to the second bag and, searching through the tissue paper, pulled out the tiny pink babygro suit and held it up in front of him.

'Mmm...' He put a finger to his lips and tapped them thoughtfully. 'So you haven't quite made up your mind.'

She couldn't help a small smile. Somehow whenever she thought of their baby she felt her spirits lift in hope. She was bonded with Xavier by the presence of their growing foetus, a bond that no human signature could take away.

'I'm not committing myself either way just yet,' she answered.

'What about dinner?' he asked. 'Have you made up your mind about that?'

She didn't have time to think of an excuse even if she'd wanted one. The truth was she wanted to spend the evening with him. She wanted to spend the rest of her life with him, but how could she tell him that now?

'Where were you thinking of going?' she asked, hoping she sounded casual and uninterested.

'What say I surprise you?'

She made her way to the stairs, scooping up her purchases on the way past.

'Give me ten minutes?' she tossed over her shoulder.

'Five.'

'Seven.'

'Four.'

'I need more time!'

'What for?' he asked. 'You look beautiful as it is. I like your hair by the way; did you have it done?'

She wished she could have some device installed in her system to stop her being so ridiculously affected by his compliments.

'Yes…'

'You've got three minutes left,' he told her, the edge of his mouth lifting again in that stomach-flipping smile.

She turned and scooted up the stairs.


Carli was completely shocked by his choice of restaurant. The décor had changed but it was still recognisable as the very first restaurant they'd gone to as a new couple when they'd first met.

She didn't know what to make of it. Was he intentionally reminding her of what they'd shared in the past?

She waited until they were seated to ask, 'Why are we here?'

'Why not here?' He gave her an unreadable glance as he reached for the menu.

She bent her head to her own menu, her thoughts flying off in all directions.

It had been their favourite restaurant.

He'd taken her here for their first date, they'd celebrated

their first month together here, they'd celebrated their second…he'd asked her to marry him on the third.

She stole a glance at him over the top of her menu but he seemed to be concentrating on the long list of foods available. She bent her head once more, trying her best not to feel emotional…but still…

The proprietor of the restaurant approached and greeted Xavier by name, and as his glance swung to Carli his eyes widened in delight.

'Carli Knightly!' he crowed. 'You are back with us.'

She wasn't sure what to say but thankfully Xavier got in first. 'Carli goes by the name of Gresham now.'

'Gresham?' Emilio frowned. 'Bah! I will always think of you as Carli Knightly. Now, what can I tempt you both with?'

Carli knew it was pointless arguing the point and quickly rattled something off the menu to keep the waiter off the subject of her divorce from who was quite clearly his most preferred client.

Xavier gave his own order and once Emilio had gone turned his gaze on her.

'Relax, Carli, you look as if you're expecting all the kitchen staff to come stomping out here to berate you for leaving me in the first place.'

'The kitchen staff didn't have to live with you—I did.'

'You seemed to enjoy it at the time.'

She could hardly argue with that. For the most part she'd been ecstatically happy living with him, sharing his life, his bed…

'It had its compensations,' she offered with an element of grudge.

His laughter sent a shiver of reaction down her spine and she reached for her water glass to disguise how much he affected her.

'In spite of my snobbish family and my selfish career?' he teased.

She gave him a short glance before inspecting the bread rolls set before them, choosing one carefully to delay her response.

'Although I've said to the contrary, in the end my leaving you really had very little to do with your family,' she said, avoiding his eyes. 'As you said once before, we were at different stages of our careers. It was never going to work; I can see that now.'

'You know something, Carli, if you go looking for failure that's exactly what you'll find. Our marriage would have worked but you didn't expect it to.'

Was it true? Had she on a subconscious level expected their relationship to fail and once it hit the first hurdle she'd left before any further damage could be done? Had she asked for a divorce because deep down she had been dreading him asking the same and she couldn't allow him to get in first?

'You seemed intent on arguing at every point over every single detail,' he continued. 'The honeymoon wasn't even over when you told me flatly you weren't having children. Can you imagine how that made me feel?'

'Maybe you should have asked me before you married me,' she said. 'Or perhaps you could have run a check-list by me to see if I was up to the task of being a suitable wife. You know, whether I wanted to give up work, how many children I wanted, that sort of thing. You could have saved yourself a whole lot of bother and moved on to the next woman who actually wanted to be a doormat for the rest of her life.'

He let out a sigh of impatience. 'When have I ever treated you as such? For God's sake, Carli, if you stay with me you'll have household help for as long as you want it.

You will be one of the few women who actually *can* have it all—the husband, the kids and the high-powered career.'

The bread roll in her grasp dropped back on her plate as her eyes went back to his.

'Husband?' she asked, frowning at him in confusion. 'But I thought you said—'

'I was speaking figuratively,' he said, shifting his gaze to the left of hers.

She hunted his face for a clue to what he was feeling but all she could see was rigidity in the set of his jaw. There was no sign of love reflected in his dark blue gaze as it clashed with hers on the way past.

He didn't want to marry her because deep down he knew the attraction they still had for each other wasn't permanent. He wanted access to his child but wasn't prepared to go to the lengths of formal commitment any more.

The irony of it was almost painful, she thought. Here she was, the ardent, career-driven feminist, wishing he would go down on bended knee and tell her he couldn't live without her.

He could easily live without her.

He had done so for five long years.

He'd quickly replaced her with an array of new lovers, each one moving aside for the next, unlike her, who, no matter how hard she tried, just couldn't let go...

'Can't you see I'm prepared to do whatever it takes to make this work?' he asked after a stiff silence.

'What a pity you didn't get it right the first time around.'

His jaw tightened as he fielded her scornful glance. 'Well, you know what they say about practising to get things perfect.'

'I'd hardly describe our relationship as anywhere near perfect,' she tossed back.

'There are times when it comes pretty damn close,' he

said. 'Think of how good we are together. You melt in my arms every time.'

'So, you're a good lover, but then no doubt your extensive practice over the past five years has paid off. Lucky me,' she drawled, reaching for her glass.

'It annoys you I've had other lovers?'

She gave her head an indifferent toss. 'Why should I care what you've been doing?'

'Why indeed?' he mused.

She fought against the urge to squirm in her seat, so agitated was she by the turn of conversation. She had to remind herself she'd been the one to leave him. Their relationship had been well and truly over. She had nailed the last nail into the coffin that contained their marriage. She had absolutely no right to feel jealous of all the women who had stepped up to take her place.

No right at all.

She met his eyes across the table, her hands tightening into two small knots on her lap. 'Was there…anyone during the last few months?'

'You mean since the night of the lift?'

'Yes…' She disguised a small swallow. 'I know it's probably none of my business but…' She lowered her gaze, unable to hold his studied look any longer.

'I could ask the same of you, of course,' he said after another pause.

'Believe me, you don't need to.' Her tone was rueful. 'I think after that night I more or less learned my lesson about one-night stands.'

'The answer is no,' he said, bringing her eyes back to his in surprise.

'No?' She swallowed again. 'Not even one?'

He shook his head.

'But…but why not?' she asked.

'I had other things on my mind.'

Emilio appeared with their food and the opportunity to question him further passed.

Carli stared at the contents of her plate as if she couldn't quite work out how they had got there. Since when had she ever eaten venison?

'Is something wrong with your meal?' Xavier asked once Emilio had left.

'No…' She picked up her knife and fork, trying not to grimace at the rich meal in front of her. 'Everything's fine…'

Xavier watched her struggle through the first three mouthfuls before laying his own cutlery down and, reaching across, quickly changed their plates over.

'What are you doing?' she asked.

'I'm saving you from the embarrassment of confronting Emilio with an untouched meal still sitting on your plate.'

She looked down at the succulent chicken breast stuffed with spinach and feta cheese he'd put in front of her and decided against defending her choice with her usual fervour.

'I think I must have misread the menu,' she said instead.

'Either that or your mind was on other things,' he offered, lifting a forkful of what had previously been her meal to his mouth.

Carli attended to the food before her, wondering what sort of things had been on his mind in the last few months since they'd run into each other at the conference.

Had he even thought about her?

Probably not, she told herself sternly, he'd promised after that one drink she'd never see him again. Even though that one drink had led to… Well, it was still no reason to think he had even once considered contacting her again.

The baby shifted inside her, the flutter of tiny limbs stalling her in the process of relaying a forkful of food to her mouth.

'What's wrong?' Xavier sent her a concerned look.

She smiled softly as the growing infant gave another reminder of its presence.

'Your baby is evidently finding its current accommodation a little cramped,' she said.

His expression softened and her stomach did another somersault, which this time had nothing whatsoever to do with the child in her womb.

'You'd better tell him it's going to get a whole lot more crowded in there in the next four months,' he smiled.

'So you think it's a boy now, do you? What happened to the little girl with curly chestnut hair and a fiery temper?' she asked.

He gave her a teasing smile. 'I've already got one of those—you. Besides, Knightlys always have sons first. It's a genetic tradition.'

Her expression told him exactly what she thought of his genetic traditions and he laughed. 'You know, I think you think it's a boy too, but you won't allow yourself to agree with me on anything on principle.'

'I don't have to agree with you if I don't want to.'

'No, of course you don't, but I have a gut feeling on this.'

'Does your gut feeling stretch to possible names?' She picked up her fork once more and resumed eating.

'I've been thinking about it over the last few weeks,' he said. 'We should buy one of those baby-name books and go over it together.'

Carli suppressed a tiny sigh. Anyone listening in could easily think they were a happily connected couple excitedly awaiting the birth of their first child. If it hadn't been for their accidental pregnancy she would quite probably be sitting alone right now in her flat, watching something inane on the television as she had done for the past five years, while he would have been out with his latest lover.

'Were you going to keep your promise?' she asked into the silence that had fallen once their plates were cleared from the table.

He pressed his napkin to the corner of his mouth before responding. 'Which promise was that?'

'The one about never seeing me again.'

He gave a slight frown as he rearranged his napkin across his lap, but when his gaze meshed with hers his expression was mask-like once more.

'I'm known to be a man of my word, or have you forgotten?'

It wasn't quite the answer she'd been searching for.

'I'm not sure I know you all that well any more,' she said, a small frown taking up residence between her brows. 'In fact, I often wonder if I knew you properly in the first place.'

'You could be right.' He gave her another one of his quick, unreadable glances. 'I've never been particularly comfortable with revealing all my cards. I guess you could say that was one lesson my nanny taught me well.'

'What was she like?' Carli asked softly, almost tentatively.

He gave one of his indifferent shrugs. 'You're familiar with the type; in fact when I first met your elderly neighbour I thought it was Nanny Tipple all over again.'

'Was that her real name?'

He gave her a twisted smile. 'No, her real name was Tipper but I renamed her after I began measuring the gin and sherry bottles in the drinks cabinet every day. She was steadily drinking her way through my parents' supply of aperitifs, not that they noticed, of course.'

Carli was well aware of the significance of his wry revelation. On the few occasions he'd mentioned his childhood, she hadn't picked up on any dissatisfaction with how things had been conducted in the Knightly household.

Had she missed something at the time?

Had she been even listening to him?

*Truly* listening?

'Did you tell your parents about what she was doing?' she asked.

'I made one or two attempts.'

'They didn't believe you?'

'They didn't want to have to go through the inconvenience of replacing her.' He leaned back in his chair with the lazy sort of grace she knew she would always associate with him and only him. 'My mother's words were, and I quote, ''I can't go through the tedious interview process again! What harm is she doing? What's a drink now and again anyway? God, if I had to mind them all the time I'd be hitting the bottle myself!'''

There was no mistaking the bitterness in his tone. Carli felt a wave of empathy rush through her at the thought of him as a young child trying to deal with the dysfunctional adults in his life, taking on responsibilities no child should have to face.

'What eventually happened?' she asked.

'One afternoon during the school holidays Imogen, my youngest sister, nearly drowned in the back-yard swimming pool.'

'Oh, my God!' Carli's face paled with shock.

'Lucky for her I was there and dragged her out.'

'You saved her life?'

He gave another could-mean-anything shrug. 'She was still breathing…but only just.'

'You should have told me…'

'Why?'

'I don't know…I just think one's wife should know of the most significant things in one's past.'

'But you're not my wife.'

Her eyes went back to his. 'No…but I was before.'

'There are things you should have told me as well, so we're more or less quits, don't you think?'

She stared at the starched whiteness of the tablecloth for a moment or two.

'You saved a life—your sister's. My mother died a lonely death while I was on school camp. It was probably my absence that killed her.'

He leant forward in his chair, almost knocking over his glass as he did so. He righted it with one hand as the other reached for one of hers, his strong fingers interlacing with her trembling ones. 'No, you mustn't think that.'

She looked down at their joined hands and sighed. 'Don't you ever wish you could roll back time?' She lifted her eyes to his and was surprised at how deep and dark his gaze had become. 'If I could just go back and tell her how much I loved her maybe she wouldn't have done what she did.'

'You shouldn't be blaming yourself,' he said huskily. 'Not after all this time.'

'If Imogen had died, wouldn't you have done the same?'

His fingers around hers tightened momentarily. 'I think I'm going to have to be very careful around you in future.' His mouth bent into a rueful smile. 'You're starting to get to know me too well.'

She smiled back at him, somehow feeling closer to him than she'd ever felt before, even during the time they were married.

'Do you think we'll be good parents?'

'The best,' he said with a confidence she privately envied. 'We're aware of all the mistakes, so hopefully we won't make them.'

A shadow of doubt passed over her face as she looked down at their joined hands once more.

'It would be so much better if things were…more normal between us.'

'Hey.' He reached over the table and lifted her chin so her eyes had to meet his. 'What we have is normal, don't ever forget that. We're attracted to each other in spite of the past. I want you and you want me—what more could we ask? Didn't the little kitchen routine demonstrate that?'

She gave him what she hoped was a convincing smile.

What she wanted was out of reach and the irony was she had been the one to push it even further away. The only thing connecting them now was their desire for each other and the baby that had been conceived out of that need.

'Do you want dessert?' she asked, picking up the menu Emilio had discreetly placed at her elbow, perusing its contents with pretended avid intent.

Xavier frowned as he bent his head to the menu card in his hand. What he wanted wasn't printed on the menu; it was sitting right in front of him.

'I think I'll give it a miss.' He placed the menu to one side.

'What about Emilio?' she asked. 'Aren't you concerned about offending him?'

'I think he'll understand the direction my appetite has taken.'

Carli's menu fluttered to the table from her suddenly nerveless fingers as her eyes met his across the short distance of their table.

'You want to go home?' she asked in a breathless whisper.

'You bet I do,' he said and his chair scraped back as he got to his feet, his hand reaching across the table to link once more with hers.

# CHAPTER NINE

CARLI sat beside him in the car on the journey home, her senses already spinning out of control by the gleam of rampant desire she'd seen reflected in his eyes as they left the restaurant.

Although the trip back to Mosman was no great distance from Paddington, and the traffic on the Harbour Bridge more or less moving freely, she still felt as if they were crossing the entire continent.

She was intensely aware of him beside her, his long-fingered hands on the steering wheel, his midnight-blue gaze fixed on the road ahead. She could see the bunching of muscles in his left thigh as he shifted the gears and had to fight with herself not to reach out and run her fingers along the hard length of his leg.

She tightened her hands in her lap and stared fixedly ahead, wondering if he could sense her anticipation. She knew he was going to make love to her, knew it with every pulsing nerve in her body. She could even feel her body prepare itself intimately and squeezed her thighs together, her heart doing a funny little skip in her chest as she thought about how he would soon reach for her.

The sensor lights came on as they drove into the driveway and she forced her breathing under some semblance of control. She watched as Xavier came around the front of the car to open her door, an action she had in the past berated him for, claiming herself perfectly able to open a door for herself.

Where were all her ideals now?

The door opened under his hand and she eased herself out with as much grace as she could, considering the jelly-like state of her legs.

The garage was spacious but because she'd parked her car crookedly earlier she found herself far too close to his body as she straightened.

He leaned past her to close her door, bringing his chest into contact with hers in a brief but burning brush of flesh on flesh.

His eyes met hers in the dim lighting.

She felt her indrawn breath stall somewhere in her throat as he leaned her back against the car, the cold metal at her back in sharp contrast to his body's warmth at her front from chest to thigh.

His mouth came down and claimed hers in a kiss that spoke of his urgent need, the same urgent need his lower body was making more than clear where it probed against her.

She felt the unfolding of his tongue against hers, the slight grazing movement stirring her into a frenzy of passionate yearning for more of his touch. Her flesh was tingling where his hardness imprinted her softness, the swell of their child between them only intensifying the need to get even closer.

His mouth became even hungrier and demanding upon hers, his hands moving from where he'd been leaning them against the car to slide up her arms and then to where her breasts lay aching for his possession.

The thin fabric of her dress was shifted aside to give him access to the pointed bud of her nipple, his warm tongue moving over its engorged peak in a caress of such intoxicating pleasure a whimpering cry burst from her lips before she could control it.

He moved to her other breast, the sweep of his tongue

sending her senses into a tailspin, her brain emptying of everything but the need for him to possess her totally.

Her hands went to his belt but he stalled the movements of her frantic fingers with one large hand.

'No.' His breathing was ragged. 'Not here. Let's go upstairs.'

She wanted him now, right here and now before he changed his mind.

She unpeeled his fingers from over hers and attacked his buckle once more, this time succeeding. She heard his sharply indrawn breath as her fingers slid beneath the straining fabric of his under-shorts, a little smile playing about her mouth when his fullness was released into her hand.

'You're one determined woman, do you know that?' he growled down at her playfully.

'You'd better believe it.' She moved her hand in slow motion, glorying in the tortured pleasure playing out on his features as he fought with himself to keep control.

He sucked in another breath and, pushing her hand away, leaned her back against the car, his hand searching for the hem of her dress.

She felt the brush of his hand along her thigh as he slid her panties away, and her breathing hastened almost painfully as his hands gripped her hips to position her for his entry.

The smooth, hard glide of his body within hers sent all the breath out of her lungs in a harsh sigh of relief. This was where she wanted him!

She could tell he was trying to restrain himself but she wouldn't let him drop his pace, clutching at him, her fingers digging into the tautness of his buttocks to bring him even deeper into her silky warmth.

She heard him mutter a short, sharp swear word before

he finally caved in with a great surging movement that arched her back hard against the car. His deep thrusts brought her closer and closer to the highest point of pleasure, all of her sensitive nerves tightening in preparation for the final fling into paradise. She sensed his own need for release gathering behind his stronghold like flood waters behind a sandbank; within a few seconds all would be released in a great wash of feeling, sweeping both of them away on its raging tide.

She felt the first ripple and gasped as the second came hard on its heels, plunging her over the edge of reason into the swirling vortex of rapture, the aftershocks of her pleasure causing him to finally lose control.

She felt the exultation of his release both inside and out, her flesh shivering in vicarious delight at the sound of his deep, agonised groans as he sank against her in ecstasy.

She didn't want to move.

She wanted to hold him within her, to feel his warmth, the stickiness of his life force anointing her like a sacred balm.

Words of love hovered on her tongue, but before she could even rehearse them mentally he stepped away from her, his action releasing her bunched-up dress, its soft folds skimming over her still sensitive skin as the fabric fell in a silky silence around her knees.

He readjusted his clothing with the sort of casual ease she envied, particularly as her panties were still on the floor at her feet.

As if he had read her mind he bent and scooped them up and handed them to her. 'Yours, I believe?'

She took them and scrunched them into a ball in her hand, her eyes skittering away from his, for once unable to think of a single thing to say.

She felt rather than saw him smile.

'Don't look so ashamed, Carli; you were supposed to enjoy yourself.'

A flash of resentment lit her gaze as it collided with his. How like him to cheapen what they'd shared as if it meant nothing to him.

'I hope you, too, were suitably entertained?' she returned.

'Everything about you entertains me, Carli,' he said, 'absolutely everything.'

'Glad to be of service.' She made to brush past but he stuck out an arm like a crossing barrier, blocking her exit.

'Whoa there, sweetheart.' He turned her back to face him. 'What's going on?'

'Nothing.' She tried to release herself but his hold remained firm.

'You're shutting me out again.'

'*I'm* shutting you out?' She gave him a heated glare. 'Haven't you got that around the wrong way? You're the one who trivialises it every time we…we…'

'Make love,' he filled in for her, letting go of her arm.

'Have sex. We have *sex,* Xavier.' She dusted off her arm as if he'd contaminated it. 'We do not make love.'

'Sex, then; I'm not all that particular over the terms.'

'And I suppose you're not all that particular over your partners either,' she shot back.

'I don't know about that, and as for trivialising what we share that's only because even after all this time I still don't know what the hell to do about you.'

She opened and closed her mouth on the stinging retort she'd prepared, his wry confession throwing her off course.

'The truth is, Carli,' he continued heavily, 'I don't think I can handle this…arrangement we have too much longer.'

Carli felt her stomach roll over in panic.

He wanted out.

In spite of the baby she carried he wanted to get out of her life—for good.

No wonder he hadn't insisted on their remarrying.

'If you remember, I never wanted this ''arrangement'' in the first place,' she said, carefully avoiding his eyes.

'I know and that's what eats at me the most. I forced you back into my life in more ways than one, and now I have to live with the consequences.'

She stole a look at his expression but had to accede he was too damn good at keeping his cards close to his chest. No wonder he'd built the reputation he had legally. No one, but no one, could read him.

'Maybe we need some time out,' she said with the sort of emotional detachment she'd heard him use countless times. 'I could stay with Eliza; help her get on her feet for a couple of days.'

He frowned and opened his mouth to tell her no, but she'd already moved beyond his reach, her staccato footsteps as she made her way towards the house echoing through the still air of the summer evening.

He turned and snapped off the garage light with a savage movement of his hand, the sudden darkness reminding him of the last five years without the love of his life.

He heard the front door open as she entered the house but still he didn't move.

He stared at his car parked far too close to hers and sighed, the rush of air almost painful as it passed through his chest.

He still loved her.

There, he'd said it. Admitted it to himself at last.

When had he not loved her? Who had he been kidding? Hadn't the past five years taught him anything?

Without her he was only half alive. Going to the conference had taught him that. As soon as he'd seen her he'd gone into overdrive emotionally, his only choice at the time to shut down in case he inadvertently revealed his feelings. The only trouble was his feelings had found another outlet. He'd virtually poured himself into her, making her pregnant in the process.

Maybe he'd done it subconsciously, his body deciding it was time to lay down his genes with the partner of his choice in an action described by scientists as purely instinctive.

The only trouble was his instincts told him she was unhappy. She hadn't wanted children in the first place. How could she possibly be happy now, carrying his child?

She'd left him five years ago, insisting on an immediate divorce. She'd walked away from him and never looked back, except perhaps in anger.

Yes, he'd been selfish career-wise but that too had been more or less instinctive, not that it was any sort of excuse, but the patterns of his family had been set down just as immutably as hers, although it was a great pity it had taken him this long to see it. Running the family law firm had been bred into his blood and, like his father and grandfather before him, he thrived on the pressure. Carli had got caught in the crossfire of his push for a place in the legal world but he hadn't realised it until it was too late.

He turned to look at the house, the lights inside like golden eyes looking back over the past.

He still remembered the sound of her happy laughter as he'd carried her over the threshold that first time, and the way her arms had linked around his neck as if she was never going to let go.

Her caramel-brown eyes had shone with love for him then, but within a year instead of love he'd begun to see them flash with anger instead. The arms that had held him close had begun to push him away, the words of her affection had turned to vitriolic exchanges, most of which he'd managed to sort out in bed, but towards the end even that hadn't worked.

He still found it painful to recall that last argument. Anger wasn't an emotion he'd seen demonstrated all that often during his childhood. His mother's occasional stiff silences and his father's cold, disapproving moods had been the only clues to the Knightly family boat rocking slightly as it steered a steady course towards greater and greater prosperity. He really hadn't had any idea of how to deal with flung vases, irrespective of their market value. Carli's outbursts had been disquieting to say the least.

They still were.

He could hardly blame her for being angry now. He'd railroaded her into his life with his usual heavy-handedness, not stopping to think of what she wanted or needed. She needed independence but how was he helping her by tying her to him in such a way? He had to show her he wanted what was best for her…even if it was the very worst for him…

She was packing her things with the sort of quiet determination that unsettled him even more than her fiery temper.

'Can I do anything to help?' he asked, leaning against the door jamb in what he hoped was a casual and unaffected pose.

She folded a garment roughly and stuffed it into the bag on the bed. 'No, I've just about got it covered.' She snapped the bag shut and turned to face him. 'I'm only taking the bare essentials tonight.'

He picked up the bag from the bed. 'How long will you stay with Eliza?'

She gave a noncommittal shrug as she slung her handbag

over her shoulder. 'I'm not sure…a day or two…maybe a week. I'll see how it goes.' She scooped up some cosmetics off the dresser and stuffed them into a carrier bag.

'Carli…'

She sidestepped him to retrieve a bangle she'd left hanging on one of the dressing-table drawer knobs and shoved it over her hand.

'Let's not go over the gory details of our relationship just now, Xavier,' she tossed at him without looking at him directly. 'I just couldn't bear it. I need some breathing space—we both do. Besides, Eliza and the kids could do with some company right now.'

He wanted to say he needed her company, needed it more than anything, but something told him her mood was not particularly receptive at present. Her body language was screaming at him to keep back, and her eyes in particular were deliberately avoiding his.

'As you wish,' he said stiffly and reached to hold the bedroom door for her to pass through, his dark eyes following her movements as she brushed past.

He carried her bag downstairs and, after placing it in the car, watched as she slipped behind the wheel, flicking him a quick glance from beneath her curtain of hair as she gunned the engine.

'I'll call you,' she said, tucking a chestnut lock behind one ear.

He stepped away from the car, thrusting both hands in his pockets to stop them from reaching in and snatching the keys out of the ignition.

'You know where to find me.' He stripped his tone of all emotion.

She didn't answer other than to reverse out of his garage, which seemed to him to be an answer in itself.

Her car hit the kerb with an ignominious bump and rattled off down the street as he stood like one of his priceless marble statues, his frozen gaze following her departure.

Carli could barely see for tears. She didn't stop to brush them away from her eyes until she was well clear of the house. She didn't want Xavier to think she was cut up about leaving him for a few days; her battered pride would just not allow it.

She turned the corner and a huge sob escaped closely followed by another. She allowed herself half the journey to Eliza's house to cry, but at the halfway point she dragged herself together with a mammoth effort and by the time she pulled into her friend's driveway her eyes, though red, were now dry.

'What the hell are you doing here at this time of night?' Eliza asked as she opened the door to see Carli standing on the doorstep, bag in hand.

'I thought you might need some company.'

'Has Xavier kicked you out?'

'No…I just felt we needed some breathing space for a few days.'

Eliza took her bag and kicked the door shut with her foot as she ushered her in. 'Well, I won't tell you I told you so.'

'Thanks, I'd really appreciate it.'

'You look exhausted,' Eliza said. 'Do you want to talk about it?'

Carli gave her a watery smile. 'I'd like to go to bed; do you mind?'

'Of course I don't mind,' Eliza said. 'But just answer this: does this mean you're thinking about re-subscribing to the all-men-are-a-complete-waste-of-time club?'

'No…not exactly.'

'Did you have some sort of showdown with Xavier?'

'No...not really.'

'Then why did you leave his house?'

Carli sank to the nearest chair with a deep sigh. 'I haven't really left. I'm just having some time out.'

'Was he getting too hot to handle?' Eliza guessed with the sort of astuteness only a long-term friend could have.

'A bit...' Carli's gaze slipped away from the close scrutiny of her friend.

Eliza gave her a long and thoughtful look.

'Have you told him how you feel about him?'

Carli shook her head. 'What would be the point? He'd feel even more pressured into a relationship; the pregnancy has been bad enough.'

'You do want this baby, don't you?'

Carli swung her gaze back to her friend's questioning one. 'Of course I do!'

'You've really changed your tack, haven't you, my girl? Where's Ms Career-Comes-First-No-Kids-No-Ties etcetera?'

Carli's shoulders slumped. 'She's long gone; in fact, I wonder if she really existed in the first place.' She examined her hands in her lap and continued, 'To tell you the truth, I can't bear the thought of going back to work next week.'

'Hasn't anyone ever told you that millions of people feel like that every single Monday morning?'

'Yes, I suppose you're right.' She gave another sad little sigh. 'I guess I never thought I'd ever crave being a wife and mother more than having a career.'

'I take it Xavier hasn't offered a rerun?'

'He did the day I told him I was pregnant but...' Her words trailed away as she thought back to that day. He had practically begged her to remarry him but she had thrown his offer back in his face. The next time the subject had come up he had changed his mind completely, telling her he had no intention of remarrying her. Had he changed his mind or had she changed it for him?

'But?' Eliza prodded.

Carli met her friend's probing gaze. 'He had second thoughts and retracted the offer.'

'I guess he isn't game to remarry you considering how it ended the last time,' Eliza commented wryly.

Carli gave an inward grimace at her friend's reminder of the bitterness of the past. She'd certainly stormed out of his life with all her feminist guns blazing.

'If he really wanted me in his life permanently, surely he would have said so by now?' she said after a pause.

'Men are strange creatures, Carli. What they say and what they actually mean can be two totally different things. Who knows what he's thinking? I haven't worked out my own husband's head, let alone that of yours.'

'Have you seen Aidan lately?' Carli snatched at the subject change with relief.

'I saw him yesterday.'

'And?'

'I told him I was unwell and now on medication for my condition.'

'What was his reaction?'

'I think he's of the wait-and-see mind set.' Her mouth twisted ruefully. 'I was quite a shrew to him for months so I can hardly blame him. But at least he didn't mention the word divorce while he was here.'

'Are you feeling any better yet?'

'It takes ages for the medication to kick in but to tell you the truth as soon as the doctor told me what was wrong I felt better. For months I thought I was losing my mind. At least now I know I'm going to get better even if it takes a while to get things on an even keel.'

'At least you've got a valid excuse for being a pain in the neck,' Carli said dispiritedly. 'I wish I had one.'

'I don't know, pregnancy is kind of a hormonal shake-up too, you know.'

'That might explain the last few weeks but it doesn't excuse what happened five years ago.'

'If you had your time over again, what would you change?' Eliza asked.

'I don't know…maybe I would have explained about my background.'

'You always were very secretive about that,' Eliza observed. 'What actually happened?'

Carli told her and when she'd finished was surprised at how much more relaxed she felt. It was as if a load had been taken off her back, a huge load she'd been trying to keep hidden even as it bent her double with the effort.

'You should have told me,' Eliza said.

'That's exactly what Xavier said.'

'Yeah, well, he of all people had a right to know. Jeepers, Carli, you were married to him, for God's sake. If you didn't trust him enough with your deepest fears, why did you marry him in the first place?'

Carli compressed her lips as she thought about how to answer. She had loved him both wildly and desperately. She'd given him her body and her heart but not her trust. She'd kept that part of herself separate, unwilling to allow another person to let her down as both of her parents had done each in their different ways.

'I guess you're right,' she said at last. 'I didn't give our marriage a chance right from the outset. Now of course it's too late, much too late.'

'It's only too late when someone dies,' Eliza said. 'Then it's truly over.'

'So you haven't completely given up hope on your relationship with Aidan?' Carli asked, looking at her intently.

Eliza gave a little shrug which spoke volumes. 'I hate using clichés but I think time is a great healer. Even a few days can make all the difference, let alone months or even years. I can't expect Aidan to walk back into my life as if nothing had happened but I can at least try to make up for the damage I've caused to our relationship, unintentional as it was.' She got to her feet and held out a hand to her. 'Come on, you've gone bug-eyed on me just like Amelia does when she's been up too long. What you need is a good night's sleep and, to use yet another cliché, things will look much brighter in the morning.'

Carli hoped she was right, but even as she lay watching the dawn sky being written on by the far-reaching golden fingers of the rising sun the next morning, she still felt as if her world was turning a gloomy grey…

# CHAPTER TEN

CARLI heard the sound of Brody crying and finally gave up on the notion of sleeping in to make up for her restless night. She padded through to the nursery and reached for him with a soft smile.

'You make an awful lot of noise for such a little person, do you know that, Brody?'

Brody smiled and tugged at her loose hair, his tiny legs wrapping around her with such snuggly warmth that a deep wave of maternal longing passed through her at the thought of her own child reaching for her in the not too distant future.

She turned to find the silent Amelia standing in the doorway, watching her steadily.

'Hi there, Princess Amelia.' Carli moved towards the door. 'Want to help me find a bottle and formula for your baby brother? I thought we should let Mummy sleep in for a while.'

Amelia led the way out to the kitchen without saying a word, even the steps she took so deliberately silent that Carli wondered yet again what was going on in that little blonde head.

Within a few minutes Brody was happily sucking on his bottle while Amelia pushed a few spoonfuls of cereal to her mouth, her big blue eyes so serious it pained Carli to look into their solemn depths.

'My daddy doesn't live here any more,' Amelia announced into the silence.

Carli wasn't sure how to manage such a blunt statement from one so young. 'I…I see.'

'He doesn't love us any more.'

'Darling, I'm sure he still loves you…he's just…' Her reply trailed off at the cynicism in the blue-eyed stare coming her way.

'Do you think it's my fault?' the little girl asked.

'Of course it's not your fault!' Carli placed Brody in his high chair and came to squat down beside Amelia's chair, taking her hand in hers and stroking it affectionately and, she hoped, reassuringly. 'Mummy and Daddy need some time to sort things out, that's all. It's nothing to do with you or even Brody. You must always remember that.'

'Is Mummy going to die?' The china-blue eyes shone with brimming tears.

'No, darling girl, she's not going to die. She's taking some special tablets to make her well but it's going to take some time for them to work. She'll be as good as new soon.'

'Will Daddy come back then?'

Carli swallowed. 'I don't know… Why don't we just wait and see?'

Amelia released herself from Carli's embrace and jumped down off her chair. 'Can I watch TV now?'

Carli straightened and smiled. 'Of course you can, but only if Brody and I can join you.'

The little mouth stretched into a semblance of a smile. 'I'd like that. Mummy never has time to watch it with me. Do you like *The Wiggles*?'

'I just love *The Wiggles*,' Carli said and, scooping up the baby from his chair, followed the little girl to the lounge room, her own spirits lifting in response to Amelia's.

An hour or so later Eliza found the three of them cuddled

up on the sofa, her daughter's delighted giggles having woken her.

'Sorry to leave you to babysit.' She gave her tousled hair a rough comb with her fingers. 'I slept so deeply last night. I didn't even wake once.'

'Good for you,' Carli said. 'It's exactly what you needed. Can I get you some breakfast?'

'Hey, you're the house guest not the housekeeper.' Eliza gave a mock-frown as she took the baby from her lap.

'I'm enjoying myself.' Carli got to her feet. 'Will you excuse me, Amelia?' she addressed the little girl. 'I'm going to have a cup of coffee with Mummy in the kitchen; call me if you need anything.'

'OK,' Amelia smiled and turned back to the television.

Eliza gave Carli a grateful look as they made their way to the kitchen. 'I haven't seen her smile in weeks,' she said. 'What did you do?'

'Nothing.' Carli reached for the kettle and filled it before continuing, 'She just needed a little reassuring, that's all.'

Eliza placed Brody back in his high chair and gave him a toy to play with, stopping to ruffle his golden curls.

'I know she misses Aidan,' she said, still with her back to Carli. 'But I can hardly bribe him to come back by using the children, can I?'

'No…I guess not,' Carli answered as she reached for two cups. She spooned instant coffee into both and turned to look at her friend. 'What you need is some time with him one on one to talk about things.'

'I can't remember the last time we had time together without one or both of the kids there,' Eliza said sadly, turning around to face her. 'But he'll never agree to go out with me now.'

'Then we won't tell him it's you he's going out with.' Carli's eyes twinkled with mischief.

'What do you mean?'

'Watch and learn,' she said, reaching for the telephone. 'What's his mobile number?'

Eliza rattled it off automatically.

'Aidan?' Carli sent Eliza a quick encouraging glance as he picked up. 'This is Carli—er—Gresham here.'

There was a tiny pause before Aidan responded, 'Long time no hear, Carli.'

'Yes…' She pressed her lips together momentarily. 'I…I was wondering if I could talk to you about something…'

'Look, I've got enough problems of my own without getting involved with what's going on between you and Xavier,' he said before she could explain. 'What is going on, by the way? I hear you're having his baby. Is it true?'

'Yes…it's true.'

'I hope things work out for you, Carli, I really do, but have you any idea of what you're letting yourself in for?'

'I think so.'

'You'd better because kids change everything and before you know it you're looking at a perfect stranger across the breakfast table, wondering what you ever had in common with them in the first place.'

'Actually, that was what I wanted to talk to you about,' she said. 'I was wondering if you would be free for dinner tonight.'

'Dinner?'

'You have to eat, don't you?' she said, winking at the hovering Eliza.

'Yes, but I don't think Xavier would—'

'Let's not bring Xavier into this. Are you free tonight or not?'

'Where were you thinking of going?' he asked after another small pause.

She named a well-known restaurant on the waterfront in

The Rocks and crossed her fingers at Eliza as she waited for his response.

'All right,' Aidan said at last. 'I'll meet you at seven. In the bar.'

'Great; thanks, Aidan, I really appreciate it.'

She put the phone down after a short exchange of desultory pleasantries and gave Eliza a victory sign in the air.

'You, my girl, are going on a date.'

'I've got nothing to wear!' Eliza's hands flew to each side of her face.

'So? We'll go shopping and get something.'

Eliza's thin shoulders slumped. 'But what about my hair?'

'That's what hairdressers are for. Now, stop looking for excuses and drink your coffee because we've got a big day ahead of us.'

Carli stood back and looked at her friend just after six pm that evening and smiled with satisfaction. 'You look fantastic, Eliza. Like a million dollars in fact.'

Eliza grunted as she ran her hands down the calf-length carmine creation that skimmed her too slim build. 'You mean we just spent a million dollars.' She put a hand to her hair uncertainly. 'You don't think it's a little…you know…too over-the-top?'

Carli put her hands on her hips in a reproachful pose. 'Where is the girl who used to be the life of every party? Come on, Eliza, this is your chance to show Aidan you're still the woman he fell in love with all those years ago.' She handed her the car keys and ushered her to the door. 'Now, get out and have a good time.'

'He'll probably storm out as soon as he sees it's me and not you.'

'Tell him I had a last-minute change of plan.'

'God, I can't believe I'm even doing this,' Eliza said as she checked her appearance once more in the hall mirror.

'Go!'

'All right already.' Eliza spun for the door. 'I'm going, I'm going.'

Carli watched as she drove away and, crossing her fingers, prayed for a miracle.

'Mummy looked like a princess,' a little voice said from just behind her.

Carli turned and smiled at Amelia. 'She did, didn't she?' She took the little girl's hand and gave it a tiny squeeze. 'Now, what was that you said about me watching your favourite DVD with you?'

Both the children were soundly asleep when Carli made herself a hot drink later that evening. She had only just put it down on the coffee-table when the door bell rang. Uncertain of who to expect at that hour, she peered through the curtains first to see if she could see who had arrived, her heart doing an instant somersault in her chest when she saw a shiny new top-of-the-range BMW parked outside.

Xavier stood in the door frame, seeming to take up all the available space in it as he looked down at her.

'Hi.'

'Hi.' She moved aside to let him in, closing the door softly behind her.

'Are the kids asleep?'

She nodded. 'Out for the count.' She twisted her hands together for an awkward moment. 'Eliza's not here but would you like a hot drink? I've not long boiled the kettle.'

'I know Eliza's not here.'

She blinked up at him. 'Y...you do?'

A small smile lifted the edges of his mouth. 'You're

really far too young and far too gorgeous to be playing the role of fairy godmother, you know.'

Her heart tripped over at his description of her as gorgeous, especially since she was still wearing a considerable portion of Brody's supper all over her cotton top.

'How did you know?'

'Aidan sent me a phone text.'

'Was he very angry?' Her shoulders shrank as she grimaced.

'I wouldn't have described it as angry,' he said, 'more gobsmacked.'

She bit her lip in sudden consternation. 'I hope I haven't made things a whole lot worse.'

'Well, she's not home yet so things must be going OK so far,' he pointed out.

'I had to do something…' She looked back up at him. 'She loves him so much and the children are missing him dreadfully, especially Amelia.'

His dark eyes held hers for a fraction longer than necessary.

'They have to work it out for themselves; no one else can do it for them.'

'I know…' She lowered her gaze. 'I just wish someone had…' She stopped mid-sentence, surprised at how close she was to revealing her regrets over the collapse of their own relationship.

'Had what, Carli?' he prompted softly.

'Nothing…' She turned away for the kitchen. 'I'll re-boil the kettle so you can—'

He caught the back of her top and brought her up against him, turning her to face him. 'Tell me what you were going to say.'

She ran her tongue over her dry lips.

'Tell me, Carli,' he repeated, 'what did you wish some-one had done?'

She looked up at him without bothering to disguise her inner yearning. 'I wish…I wish that someone had told me how differently I'd feel the morning after the divorce.'

She saw his expression soften, saw too the way his eyes darkened with emotion. 'You regretted our divorce?' he asked, his hands tightening where they rested on her shoulders.

She couldn't stop her eyes from brimming with unshed tears. 'From day one.'

'Oh, baby,' he groaned as he pulled her into his chest, one of his hands going to the back of her head, his fingers threading through the silky strands of her hair. 'I regretted it too. You have no idea how much. Every day since, I've longed to see you, touch you, make love to you, and even argue with you if only I could have you with me.'

She eased herself away to look up at him. 'You don't hate me?'

He shook his head.

'Not even a little weeny bit?'

'Nope.'

Her fingers found the hem of his breast pocket and plucked at it absently. 'So…if you don't hate me, what exactly is it you feel for me?'

He smiled down at her. 'You mean you haven't guessed?'

Hope fluttered like a mad thing in her chest. 'You're not all that easy to read…' she began. 'But I was hoping you…' Her words died away once more.

'Hoping I'd what?'

She took a deep breath and met his eyes. 'I was hoping you loved me, just a tiny weeny little bit.'

'Well, then, you're in for a big disappointment,' he said soberly.

She stared at him, trying to decipher his expression. 'I...I am?'

'I don't love you a little weeny bit at all,' he said.

'You...you don't?'

He shook his head. 'I love you to distraction. When our marriage broke up I convinced myself I no longer felt anything for you but the last few months have taught me how wrong I was. I don't think I've ever stopped loving you.'

She gaped at him in a combination of relief and wonderment. 'You're not just saying that because of the baby, are you?'

'The baby is the best thing that could ever have happened to us,' he said. 'What else would have made us see each other again? We were both so proud and stubborn and independent. You wanted what you wanted and I didn't just want what I wanted—I took what I wanted without even considering you at all.'

'No, it wasn't your fault,' she said. 'I was way too idealistic back then. I hardly knew what it was that I wanted myself.'

'Do you know now?'

She gave him a soft smile as she nestled closer. 'I know I want you, that sort of goes without saying. I also know I want our baby, but as for my career...'

'What if I offered you a partnership?'

She blinked up at him in shock. 'You mean that?'

'I know it probably reeks of nepotism but I quite fancy the idea of you working in the firm with me. We could rename it Knightly and Gresham and Associates. What do you think?'

'I think your father is going to have a heart attack when he finds out you've handed a partnership to your ex-wife.'

'Ah, but you won't be my ex-wife,' he said confidently. She looked at him in confusion. 'But…'

'Marry me, Carli.'

'You want to marry me again?' She looked at him in surprise.

'I do. As soon as I can arrange it, in fact.'

She smiled at him with eyes alight with happiness. 'I can't believe I'm hearing this… You have been so distant…so mocking and—'

'Please don't remind me how badly I've handled our relationship. That's one thing the last five years has taught me if nothing else. I guess I thought if I threw a whole lot of worldly goods your way you'd be happy. My father had done that for my mother and she seemed happy with the arrangement, but of course you were nothing like my mother. How wrong was I?'

'I was just as wrong,' she said. 'I should have told you about my family circumstances. I kept so much from you. I didn't trust you enough with the biggest issues of my life.' She took a shaky little breath and continued, 'I didn't even really mean it when I said I wanted a divorce. I was being childish and provocative but I was too proud to back down. Can you ever forgive me?'

'Only if you forgive me for not trying to talk you out of it,' he said. 'I should have realised how my family were making things so difficult for you but I just didn't see it at the time. When we talked that day in the lift I started to realise how little we'd known of each other. I wanted to call you afterwards but I kept remembering how I'd promised I wouldn't contact you. That was the deal, remember? One drink, and over and out?'

'You must have got an awful shock when I turned up at your office that day.' She smiled up at him.

'Shock?' He gave her a theatrical grimace. 'My secretary

is still talking to everyone about it. I'll have to pay her more to shut her up.'

Carli couldn't help giggling. 'I think I'm going to like working for you. It will be fun watching you being pulled into line by two women.'

'And if we ever have a daughter…' He kissed the tips of each of her fingers in turn, his eyes never leaving hers. 'Do you have any idea of what you've started, young lady?'

Her smile was nothing more than radiant. '*I've* started? What about what you've done?'

'What have I done?' His tone was all affronted innocence.

She placed his hand over the swell of her belly.

'Oh…' He grinned. 'That.'

'Yes, that.'

'I hope you're not going to hold it against me for the rest of our lives,' he said.

'No.' She pressed her abdomen against him and looped her arms around his neck. 'Only for the next four months. Is that all right with you?'

His dark eyes softened as they took in her uptilted features. 'That's perfect with me, absolutely perfect,' and he bent his head towards hers.

# EPILOGUE

CARLI and Xavier both smiled as they came back into Eleanor and Bryce's lounge room to find an array of toys scattered all over the floor. Bryce was growling like a lion at Angus, who was cackling with delight at his grandfather, while Eleanor looked on fondly.

'Any trouble?' Carli asked her mother-in-law.

'No, he's been an angel. He's very well-behaved for a not-quite-two-year-old. How was your dinner?'

'Fine,' Xavier said, scooping up his son and holding him close. 'We have some news.'

Bryce came and stood beside his wife, his arm going around her waist in a gesture of affection that still moved Carli deeply. How had one tiny child made such a difference to so many lives?

'We're having another baby,' Xavier announced proudly.

'Wonderful!' Eleanor clasped her hands together in delight. 'Did you hear that, darling? Another grandchild.'

Bryce beamed, and, reaching for his son's hand, grasped it in both of his before turning to Carli and hugging her briefly, but no less warmly.

Eleanor moved from kissing Xavier to embrace Carli, no sign of the coolness and formality of years gone past. It had taken a few months and the birth of Angus to melt the chill but Carli was glad she'd insisted on Xavier restoring some sort of peace with his parents. They hadn't come to the wedding but that had hardly mattered to Carli. She'd only wanted one person there anyway, and he'd come with a huge smile on his face which had taken her breath right away.

She looked at him now as he talked with his parents, his son in his arms, a smile of deep contentment on his face.

'Mummee, Gandad said we going to the zoo to see the lions!' Angus wriggled out of his father's arms to reach for her, pressing a wet kiss on her cheek as she gathered him close.

'What does the lion say, Angus?' Bryce held up his hands like paws and growled deep in his throat. 'Roaarrrrrh!'

Angus chuckled and buried his head into his mother's neck.

Carli exchanged amused glances with Xavier.

His smile was for her and for her alone. She knew its silent message as surely as if he'd roared it out loud.

It said: I love you.

# HARLEQUIN *Presents*

**EXPECTING!**

**She's sexy, successful
and pregnant!**

Share the surprises, emotions,
drama and suspense as our
parents-to-be come to terms
with the prospect of bringing a new life into the world.
All will discover that the business of making babies
brings with it the most special joy of all....

# THE SICILIAN'S
# DEFIANT MISTRESS
## by Jane Porter

Tycoon Maximos Borsellino made a deal with Cass for
sex. Now that Cass wants more from him, he ends the
affair. Cass is heartbroken—worse, she
discovers she's pregnant....

**On sale this February.**

**www.eHarlequin.com**

# HARLEQUIN *Presents*

## The Arranged Brides

Settling a score—and winning a wife!

**Don't miss favorite author Trish Morey's brand-new duet**

## PART ONE: STOLEN BY THE SHEIKH

Sapphire Clemenger is designing the wedding gown for Sheikh Khaled Al-Ateeq's chosen bride. Sapphy must accompany the prince to his exotic desert palace, and is forbidden to meet his future wife. She begins to wonder if this woman exists....

**Part two: The Mancini Marriage Bargain
Coming in March 2006**

www.eHarlequin.com

If you enjoyed what you just read,
then we've got an offer you can't resist!

# Take 2 bestselling love stories FREE!
# Plus get a FREE surprise gift!